CLAIMING HER

THOMPSON BROTHERS
BOOK TWO

SUMMER COOPER

LOVY BOOKS

1

LAURA

I pushed myself out of bed and headed to the bathroom, groaning as a yawn cracked my jaw. I scratched through my blonde hair, not even realizing it was sticking up in all directions. I shouldn't complain, it wasn't so long ago I didn't have any at all. I never thought I'd get up again, and here I was, staring in the mirror, thankful I got to live another day.

My one-bedroom apartment and match-box bathroom was all I needed, I thought, as a sunbeam turned my hair to fire as I looked in the mirror. My hair looked like little rays of fire and it always made me grin. That was what everyone called me at the hotel: little ray of sunshine.

If only they saw me when I woke up in the mornings, I thought, they'd think the complete opposite. I looked like a mess, which would have been fine if I'd been out all night and had a man in my bed to show for it. But it had more to do with how much work I had to do than how much time I'd spent in bed.

The guests in the hotel get worse every day. Cleaning up after them gets harder by the minute. My job was never easy, but at times it feels completely out of my league.

I didn't bother taking another glance at myself in the mirror before stripping out of the t-shirt and shorts I'd slept in and under the spray of my shower. I didn't wait for the water to warm up and yelped when the freezing water hit me at first. At least it woke me up a little.

Five minutes later, I was back in my bedroom, a towel wrapped around me as I rubbed my hair dry. I found some clothes and put them on quickly, then made breakfast and sat down to eat. There was nothing exciting about my mornings, nothing at all.

I glanced down as a blob of my egg fell onto my chest. Even though it had been a while, I still couldn't get used to them. I found myself at times, wondering if someone knew the truth behind the firm globes that greeted me. My breasts. The new ones. The old ones I lost to breast cancer and had been replaced by perky new ones. Well, I'd lost one to the cancer, the other one had been operated on to make them look similar.

Whenever men's eyes rolled over them, I wondered if they knew they weren't real. Jessi, my best friend, would laugh and say men didn't care about things like that. If they did, then there wouldn't be things like Playboy which were full of them. I laughed to myself, trying to focus on the brighter side of life, the way I did back then. I quickly scraped the egg away and wiped my shirt clean.

A few minutes later, I picked up my purse and my

phone and walked out of my tiny apartment. As soon as I did, my phone rang. Jessi's name flashed on the screen.

"Hey Jessi," I chirped, a little skip in my step as I walked down the street. Hearing her name had put a smile on my face and finally getting out of the apartment made me feel better too.

The distance from my place to the hotel was short enough that I could walk, and the exercise was good for me. Though I'd be on my feet for most of the day, walking was still way cheaper than taking a taxi.

"Hey girl, where are you?" she asked through the phone, and I picked my pace a little more.

"I don't know what got into me this morning, or rather didn't get into me. I couldn't get up this morning, and now I'm running behind." My stride and skip started to turn into a mini jog as I glanced at the time.

I knew I should have told her I'd call her later so I could flat out run to the hotel, but curiosity got the better of me. So I asked what had been playing on my mind for the last couple of days. The thing that she'd been so quiet about and one thing she knew about, I was shy but I wasn't too shy to ask about her love life.

"What's going on?"

She sighed over the phone, so I figured it wasn't good news and regretted asking.

"I'm still keeping out of his way. He's a big help there. I'd rather not have another run in with him again."

"You ran into him?" I asked as I stopped dead in my tracks. There was silence. My eyes narrowed in suspicion and I forgot about my tardiness.

"Jessi," I said, my voice lowered. "Is there something you're keeping from me?" I didn't get a response. "Jessi! We're supposed to be best friends! Don't tell me you… dumped me for him!"

I finished the words with a whimper, and I heard Jessi laugh on the other end. That had me smiling.

I'm so sorry, Jessi, I thought to her silently. So sorry you have to hurt like this. Sorry, that I'm so little help to you that you don't even come to me. Sorry that all you can think about is running away.

Whether she'd put in for the transfer already, or would soon enough, I'd miss her once she was gone. Jessi thought she was good at keeping secrets but she wasn't. She felt things too strongly for that.

I'd heard the rumor about her and Trent back when we were just starting to grow to like each other. I'd dismissed the ones that said she was a gold digger. I could always ask Emily, Trent's younger sister and a friend I'd made through Jessi, but I got the sense Emily didn't know much about her elder half-brother. I couldn't exactly ask Mason, the second oldest brother.

I still didn't know just how deep their relationship had been, but the look on Jessi's face when he'd found us in the staff room that day…

Her expression had been so fucking complicated. There was hope in it, one I wondered if she knew she still felt. There was also an old wariness there like he'd been careless with her before and she was bracing herself for him to do the same to her once again. Most of all, there was so much pain—hers—and sadness for him.

It all made me very curious, but the furious and hurt look on her face after he'd left made me think better of asking.

After all, I couldn't expect her to tell me all her secrets when I was still keeping some from her myself.

"Seriously, though," I said. "You know if you need something, I'm here for you, right? You don't have to keep things to yourself. If you'd like, I could share something, and you could share something…"

"Do you mean another girl's night? Honestly, I'm not sure I can handle another night like that, Laura."

I frowned at the secrecy before me and blew out a breath to calm myself. "You know, I've been wondering this for a while, but something happened on that night, right? And don't bother trying to lie. Tell me if you've been back to your apartment since that night."

"I… was at my parents," she said hesitantly. "I'll go back to my apartment eventually, I'm just… afraid of what I'll find there."

"What could you possibly find in your apartment besides your things?" I asked with a growing suspicion.

There was a short silence. "I guess I'm trying to avoid someone," she admitted, but then she continued hurriedly. "It's nothing to worry about, though. I wanted to find Emily, so she and I could have a chat. I haven't talked to her in a while, but I think she's still busy with her dad."

"Would you rather talk to her than me?" I asked, with sadness that wasn't entirely an affectation.

"I've known her longer, and it's to do with her father.

I'm not sure if you heard, but he had a heart attack, or so my mom said."

"There were rumors," I said vaguely, figuring she didn't need to know if she hadn't heard them yet.

Hopefully, Emily hadn't heard them either, though I did want to know the source of that information when the Thompson family was pretty good at keeping their secrets under lock and key.

"It's because he's sick that his sons are all back, after all. I wanted to know if he had any plans on getting better, or if the guys will be sticking around permanently."

"Oh well," I muttered. "I guess there's plenty more of cleaning up after Mason in my future, then. Hopefully, the guy tones it down a bit." I deliberately didn't mention Trent, even though I knew he was the one son she'd have been glad not to have come back.

"He's been behaving so far, from what I've heard. Maybe he's changed?" she mused.

I chuckled. "Oh, honey, no. A guy like that wouldn't just change so much. I bet he's just biding his time. I've had too much good luck lately. Maybe it'll happen today."

"You probably just jinxed yourself."

"Better to get it over with. I'm sick of this suspense of 'will he, when will he.' Everybody's feeling it." Then I grinned. "Though I can't say I'm not looking forward to it just a little."

She hummed. "Because there's a slight chance you get to see him at least half naked? Along with some of the pretty friends he'll be dragging along with him?"

"There's definitely that," I agreed. "It makes me feel a little jealous sometimes."

Other times, it left me so angry that there were people like that, while there were people like me who struggled with everything living in the same country.

"I know the feeling," Jessi sighed. "I'm afraid I need to go, I'm even later for work now. You should probably hurry too."

At her pointed statement, I checked my watch and my eyes widened.

"Shit!" I didn't realize I'd slowed down so much while we were talking, I'd wasted more time than I'd thought. Immediately, I picked up the pace. "Will I see you today?"

"I'll be in the kitchen. If you have the time, come by. I'll have something for you."

"Thank you, Jessi! I love you!" I chirped, then hung up.

I ran most of the way, stopping when I was within sight of the staff entrance before slowing down to catch my breath. I paused outside for a moment, hoping for a good day at work, then walked in.

2

LAURA

"You're a little late today."

Janice, one of my coworkers, couldn't help but point this out. I hated her attitude; she was the kind of person who had the word negativity on her head. I felt it whenever we came into contact. She found a problem with everyone and everything, especially the staff.

We were in the staff area of the hotel, at our lockers where we were changing into our uniforms. There were only a few of us in there, which either meant most of them were already in, or most of them would be later than us.

"It's not like I'm late for the shift, anyway. I usually just get here a little earlier to eat something before I start work."

I didn't offer her any more information than that. At the end of the day, it was none of her business. Even if she felt that she was our boss, she was far from it. She wasn't simply asking what happened today, it was as if she was interrogating my movement and out of politeness, I was answering her. A trait that Jessi said I needed to get rid of because Janice wasn't into being nice. She was into trying to get us to lose our jobs. Why? No one knew and no one cared because they were starting to know what she was truly like.

"Well, if you didn't have anything to eat, you might want to do it quickly. Or not do it at all."

Her tone made me narrow my eyes. "Why?"

"So far, it's just rumor, but another maid swore she heard that Mason was preparing for another of his parties today. His friends will be arriving early, and they'll be staying well into the evening."

It was expected the moment he came here. He'd held himself back, and I wondered if Trent being around had something to do with it, what with him being the oldest of the Thompson boys and being as strict and serious about work as their father is—the total opposite of Mason the partier.

"Well, that sucks," I muttered. "But it's not like we weren't prepared for this. Let's just hope he and his friends have a little self-control after the last time. I didn't get details, but I heard his dad threw a fit because they bothered some of the guests."

"He's not around to stop him this time," Janice pointed out.

There was that. Mr. Thompson had stopped coming to work at some point, and the rumors floating around were pretty outrageous. That he had a terminal illness, that he was hitting full retirement and wanted one of his sons to take over working at the main hotel, or that he'd had a heart attack and was dying. They all explained why he'd brought all his sons home, when Trent had never even been back to Charlotte after he left over a decade ago, from what I'd heard.

I'd only just heard the truth from Jessi this morning, but there wasn't any proof so I just shrugged.

"Maybe his older brother will stop him," I suggested.

She looked doubtful, and I wasn't sure I even wanted his help after how he'd treated my friend like shit. But if it meant not having to deal with Mason's mess, I was willing to be forgiving. Just a bit.

We both went into work mode as we picked up our supplies, then moved to the staff elevators to go to our respective floors. We were supposed to go through the rooms every day, even when they were unused. We did that so the unused rooms were ready to be occupied at any time. It was extra work, but the pay was pretty good. After a year of saving, I could even move into a bigger apartment if I wanted.

The day nosedived hours later when we got the call we were all dreading. We'd only just made it back to our station on the first floor for a short rest.

"Mason is at it again," someone groaned.

"Oh, I don't think it's that bad," someone else giggled. "I wouldn't mind a show like last time."

"If that's all you're interested in, then you can do it all yourself," a third person groused.

A fourth person sighed. "They need at least a dozen of us this time. We're about that number here, so we might as well all go."

There was some more grumbling, but we all made our way back up.

Jessi was right, I thought to myself sullenly. I'd jinxed myself.

I had second thoughts about going, but this was part of the job. To be honest, I kind of agreed with the second girl. The parties Mason threw weren't usually too bad. Besides, I needed some distraction before my anxiety at my best friend's situation pulled me too far into it. As much as I wanted to, I couldn't make Jessi's choices for her, and she was a pretty reserved person to begin with, so I knew trying to butt in would backfire on me spectacularly.

"At least it was in his room, this time," an optimistic voice said. "The last time it was in one of the hotel's lounges. He's got a big suite room, but how bad could it be, right?"

With that, a few of the people in the crowd were suddenly a little brighter, and I rolled my eyes.

It was his suite, but if they were still calling a dozen of us it had to be bad. Either that or they were hoping a lot of us would get the job done quicker, so the spoiled brat could still use his room for the night instead of moving to a new one, which he'd done before.

When we finally arrived at his room, we got to see the damage. I'd dealt with him before, but even my jaw dropped.

Fuck, the place was such a mess! We might as well replace everything in there or take everything out of the room and clean the furniture outside. The smell of booze and smoke hung in the air, and there were still a few bodies sprawled all over the floor. Other people were trying to get them up and out of the room.

Seriously?! It wasn't even that late in the day yet. The sun was still up, and they were already totally shitfaced! Damn, this kid and his friends were real…

"You're going to have to leave the room with your friends for us to get to work," one of the senior maids was saying to Mason, who was draped over a couch, looking relaxed. "We won't be able to clean properly if you stay here."

Mason hummed and raised his head to look around. By then, all his friends were already out, and he looked a little surprised.

"All right," he said, heaving himself up. "Please try to be done in a couple of hours."

I frowned at him indignantly. Even with all of us, getting his room clean in only two hours would be a bit of a stretch. Not that the young heir seemed to realize.

Then my eyes widened, and a few screams went around the room. He had a blanket over him, so I hadn't even realized it, but it fell away when he stood up. Mason was standing stark naked in a room full of maids.

"Mr. Thompson!" the maid who'd been talking to him screeched and looked away as her face went a bright pink.

Mason smirked, taking his time to walk around the room and pick out his clothes. There were a few other items tossed around, probably his friends', and I wasn't sure how they were all going to be claimed. That was only a secondary thought because my mind was all on Mason right then.

Damn the guy was hot.

He was completely not my type, and with his title of "heir", way too out of my league. On top of that, he was a fucking slob and a little too free with life, his money, and his status. So whatever interest I had in him, I knew I had to kill it for my sake before it went too far. Still, my eyes kept flitting to him and away as I tried not to stare at his incredible body. There was just no way anything could work between us, even if that kindling interest was in any way returned.

It wasn't just because of the mess I saw going on between Jessi and this guy's older brother, either. Our worlds were just too far apart. Everything had fallen apart for me when I found out I was sick and I had to quit college for the sake of my health. It had been hell for me. I hadn't grown up anything beyond comfortable, but the awful hospital bills had driven me to total poverty, and that had been hard.

I'd overcome it all. A road full of pain that I never wanted to travel again, and especially not over a scummy guy. With my second chance at life came the choice that I'd live to the fullest. I dropped all the negative people in my life and vowed to look on the bright side. In no way would I go down a road that promised pain so willingly, I hadn't even had a choice the first time.

Thinking too much about it is useless, I thought to myself. It's not like this hot, twenty-five-year-old rich boy would see me as anything but a maid.

I probably jinxed myself again with that thought, I realized in the next moment.

Fully dressed, Mason made for the door to leave us maids to do our work. As he walked toward me on his way to the door, I was surprised when he met my eyes. We'd technically 'met' plenty of times before this, but I was pretty sure he hadn't noticed because he was usually suffering from a hangover or preoccupied with some woman. There was no recognition at all in his expression, but he did throw a smirk at me, even though it was a sardonic one, and I felt my heart skip a beat. Only in surprise though!

My lips twitched because I was determined not to take this kid seriously, and I followed him with my eyes as he walked past me.

"Well, damn," I muttered teasingly. "He's well-hung."

I didn't know if he heard me, but I thought there was a falter in his step. It left me with a smirk of my own. As soon as the door closed behind him, squeals and giggles, as well as a few grumblings, filled the room with the maids that had seen his little show.

All I could think of before I left work for the day, was the look Mason had given me, and exactly what it meant. If I should let it mean anything at all because suddenly, I was conflicted. No matter what, the guy was hot, and it had been a while since a guy had caught my interest.

Of all people, I thought to myself sarcastically. It just had to be him. Way to set yourself up for disappointment, Laura.

I'd just have to suffer through it and take a leaf out of Jessi's book: go the avoidance route and hope he didn't cause me any more trouble for the remainder of his stay.

3

———

MASON

She stood watching me, and I thought that she'd be embarrassed at my purposefully shocking display, like the other maids, but she was far from it. I'd heard exactly what she said too; I wasn't sure if she wanted me to hear, but I had. Either way, I knew what she said, and I felt proud at her words.

Her. The blonde-haired and blue-eyed beauty looked at me like one of the girls back in London. There, giggling beauties had flocked around me and my American accent like bees to nectar. If this one wanted to suck my cock too, then she could have done exactly that. Maybe if we'd been alone, I pondered.

She'd acted as if she was used to seeing a cock that big on any given Sunday. I knew she was impressed though, and she didn't fucking try to hide it. If I hadn't spent the night so shift-faced, and still drunk for most of the day, then I would have toyed with her. I'd have made out that I was ready to play and told the other maids to leave in a heartbeat. But I was fucking knackered, and I had too much work to do. Nothing got in the way of working.

Fucking.

Drinking.

Even the odd joint.

Nothing.

I should treat my body like a temple. I used to when I was going to be a professional rugby player, but Dad took away the idea of that ever being a reality. The career I hoped to have one day became a distant memory the moment I started to work for the hotel.

And after all that, Dad still treated me as if I'm the paid help, even though I gave up my career to take work at one of his hotels. He'd held my inheritance over my head, which I think was a lie. It was all going to go to Trent, wasn't it?

All Dad does is compare me to my older half-brother, so when he summoned us to come back home I needed a party to get me in the mood. Usually, I partied and fucked, but I didn't always drink as much as I did last night. Coming back home always had a habit of winding me up.

I always ended up feeling like a loser even though I knew the rest of the world didn't see me that way. Self-doubt would enter in and I'd feel it like a fucking mosquito buzzing in my ear. No matter how many times I waved it out of the way like I did when I was bombarded by those little bastards when I went to visit Ghana. The fucking things bit my face, and I was lucky that I took my malaria tablets.

I hesitated as I stood by the door, wondering if I should

ask her if she wanted to know what my cock would feel like in her pussy. I'd be happy to oblige. I bet her pussy was sweet.

Why did she look familiar, I wondered. Had I seen her before?

I was shit at names but good with faces.

I shook my head as I hovered at the door. I didn't want to leave. Dad had summoned us to get together, all my siblings were going to be there, and no amount of partying had put me in the mood to deal with it. The maid wasn't my type; her eyes were sea blue, and she had light blonde hair. The type that was too innocent, especially with her small frame, but she had perky tits. Those caught my eye the moment I saw her, and as I thought about going to the family home, I suddenly found myself licking my lips thinking about my tongue all over her erect nipples.

My phone buzzed, drawing my attention away from the blonde's nipples.

"Sis!" I blurted as soon as I saw her name flash on my cell. I knew Emily was calling me to find out where I was and to make sure I was on my way.

"Mason, I'm just calling to tell you not to bother coming." Emily sighed on the other side of the line.

I stood in confusion, wondering if today I was going to be playing with the staff, something that was against my code, but Dad was pissing me off before I'd even managed to see him. I would forget about all types of code if Dad continued to piss me off, and just go for the one thing that I was in dire need of right now, and that was sex. Last night I was too wound up by him summoning us here that I didn't get any. I was so fucking horny that jerking off wouldn't satisfy me right now.

"Did you hear me?"

I was standing by the elevator with my phone in my hand, wondering whether to make the journey or not, but I could tell Emily calling to tell me not to bother meant that she wanted me to come. Quickly, too. She was my sister and maybe the only woman I ever really talked to because there weren't any other women in my life who acted as a friend or as if they even cared, only her.

"Emily. What's happened?"

"Dad's acting weird. He asked you all to come here, and now he doesn't want to see you."

Shit, he's up to his old tricks again.

"Mason, I'm worried that something's wrong," she whispered, and then I could hear her footsteps. Emily loves to wear heels and I often tease her about how she loves to make an entrance. I'm sure that's the only reason she wears them; well that and the fact that she hates being so short.

"There's always something wrong…"

She cut me off. "The thing is, Mason, it makes no sense. He asks all of you boys to be here and then the moment you are, he refuses to see you."

"That's because he's so fucking dramatic. He's always acting as if the moment he says 'jump,' we should all be asking 'how high?'"

I shook my head at the thoughts that were running through my mind. My index finger hovered near the elevator button. I hesitated, wondering whether to get the one thing that I craved right now—a taste of that maid—or go and see my dad.

Emily was still on the line and was waiting for my answer. She decided to nudge me a bit with her next words.

"Seriously, I'm scared, Mason. He's acting so… weird."

Emily's words rang through my head and made me do the one thing that I hated doing the most. The decent thing.

"Emily, I'm on my way. Don't worry, everything's going to be all right," I lied as I pressed the elevator button and thought about the incredible maid I could be pursuing right now. Sense took over because I cared too much about Emily not to make sure she was okay.

I could imagine her smile as she said, "Thanks, Mason."

"I'm getting in an elevator right now. We may lose signal. See you soon."

I hung up, not giving her a chance to reply. If I did then I'd change my mind and it was something I couldn't do. Whoever the blonde-haired, blue-eyed maid was, she'd have to wait. I had family duties to attend to, something I hated doing but knew it was the right thing to do.

As the elevator doors opened and I stepped inside, I took a deep breath to calm myself. I didn't feel cool and collected. I felt fucking angry. That was something I had to keep under wraps. I was going to make Emily feel better; I had to put my true feelings in a box. I could lock my anger up and let it back out when I was alone.

I closed my eyes as I thought about the breathing exercises I used to do before a rugby game. I was back on the field, only this time it wasn't in a sporting contest. It was a harder game, one where I was dealing with my dad which pretty much felt like the same fucking thing, but much worse. No matter what, whenever it came to him, I never felt like a winner.

4

———

MASON

I couldn't get that maid out of my mind, which was fucking weird because I wasn't the type of guy to be pining over a woman. Even if her tits would fit perfectly in my hands and I could make her scream all night long, that didn't mean I'd go home and keep thinking about her. Sexually frustrated and annoyed about Emily's take on Dad's behavior was not the best way to be feeling right now, but I told Emily that I was on my way and I was a man of my word. The way the maid eyed me up and down was priceless, as if she hadn't had any in a while or maybe ever.

Thinking back to all the times I'd been to the hotel branch in Charlotte, I'd definitely seen her. She was almost always there every time I called in the maids to clean up after my infamous parties. None of them were happy with me, but she'd always give me this complicated look. I never paid her much attention, but I was pretty good with faces. It was a big help in the family business.

My phone rang, and I glanced at the screen before ignoring it. I jumped into my car and headed out of the garage before I could make a mistake and change my mind yet again about going to the family house. The call was from one of the many women I'd had fun with for a night, and there was no point in talking to her. I never bothered to hook up with any woman more than a few times, and the level of interest was never as much as what I was feeling toward that maid right now. Not that it would go anywhere, because as much as I would have loved to, I couldn't pursue it. This was just the first time I was thinking of her as a person and it was getting to me.

"I'll get over it," I said to myself, convinced it was true. If the interest didn't die down on its own, I'd just look for someone else. After all, she wasn't really my type. The kind of women I slept with were the kind of women who knew not to expect much from me. She looked like the kind who'd expect you to stick around for a while.

I may not have the same wanderlust as my little brother, Kevin, but I rarely stuck around one place for too long at a time. Partly for my job, and partly for my not-so-well-thought-out rebellion against my dad.

I took a deep breath as I paused at the gates and thought about chickening out once again. Fuck! When did I turn into a pussy? I typed in the code and as the gates opened, I took a deep breath and parked outside.

I walked out slowly and headed up the three steps into the mansion, taking my time, prolonging the time until the confrontation. I knew I couldn't stall forever, so I went to the door and opened it. I looked around, feeling some nostalgia from the good old days when I was still a kid and rugby was everything to me. Back when Dad wasn't trying to get in my way. It was just my family, and Trent wasn't even there. He'd disappeared sometime after high school, and though I'd felt bad about it at the time, a part of me had been glad because having him around was so stifling. Up until Dad started making comparisons between Trent and me, that is.

I'd wanted to tell my old man that if he missed his other son so badly, he could go look for him instead of making me fill shoes that were way too big. I hated it.

I dialed Emily's number to track her down. I didn't feel like bumping into someone unless I had to and especially not Dad, so I called her to find out what room she was in. I wanted to talk to Emily first, anyway. She was the main reason I'd come.

I wanted out of there as fast as possible. I had a sweet maid in my room and if I was out of here fast enough, I might just be able to catch her and finish what I was so tempted to start. Emily picked up on the second ring.

"I'm here already. Where are you?"

"Oh, great, you're here! Wait in the foyer for me, I'll come and get you."

She hung up on me abruptly, and I glared at my phone. Well, at least her greeting had sounded happy, even if she'd hung up on me. I sighed and made my way into the foyer and pushed the large double doors closed. I'd always hated the heavy things. They were ostentatious, ugly, and weighed far too much.

I saw Emily coming down the stairs carefully in very

high heels. I came to a stop in the foyer, and when she cleared the steps, I opened my arms wide for her to rush into them. She wrapped her arms around me, leaning against me with a sigh, and I closed my own arms around her, rocking her gently. Her face was buried in my chest, and I rested my chin on the top of her head. Even grown up and with heels on, my little sister was still tiny. Her tiny size came packaged with a lot of love though.

"Is everything okay?" I asked as I rocked her gently in my arms.

She let out a sigh and squeezed me tight for a moment. "Everything is not okay, but I'm glad you're here."

Emily pulled away from the embrace, then took my hand and tugged me behind her as she led me to one of the lounge rooms in the mansion. Most homes had a single living room and were done with it, but that wasn't nearly enough for the Thompson family mansion.

We sat on one of the couches, Emily leaning against my arm. I arched an eyebrow as I tried to read her expression. She looked kind of… sick? Or under a terrible load of stress. My sister was always a sensitive girl, but I began to worry when she started wringing her hands and sighing a lot.

"Emily, come on now, girl. Talk to me. You're starting to worry me. What's the deal? Is it Dad? Is he worse?"

"No, no," she said quickly, shaking her head. "I'm worried about him but that's not it. I'm worried about you guys more. Well, you and Kevin more than Trent, really."

"Is he around?" I asked and couldn't help but frown.

"He came down the day after I called him. Dad came

back home the same day, but he didn't want to see Trent. I'm sure Trent was angry. He's always in such a bad mood…"

I frowned at the mention of our eldest half-brother. Trent and I didn't have much of a relationship now or when we were kids. We had nothing in common besides Dad and our last name, and it was the only reason I associated with him at all, most of the time. I could attest to his surly mood because the guy was always so serious about everything. He'd been moody growing up, too. For a moment, I wondered if Dad had constantly compared him with someone like he'd done with me.

"He didn't say anything to you, did he?"

I was about to ask the real question: what did he say to upset her this time? I was being polite which wasn't like me, but Emily was in a state and I didn't want to upset her more.

"Don't worry about that," Emily said dismissively. "Most of the time I don't even register on his radar, so it's not like he has anything to say to me anyway. For which I am so fucking glad."

I frowned at her, then flicked her forehead.

"Ow!" She pulled away from me, putting a hand to her forehead and pouting at me with a betrayed look in her gaze.

"Watch your language, you're still too young for that!"

I was the one who loved to swear—maybe a little too much—but never around her. I didn't want her to have a dirty mouth like mine.

"You're too funny. You act as if I'm a child," she said. "I can drink and drive if I want to."

I caught her cheeks in a pinch, ignoring her when she made noises about it.

"You better stick to drinking wine and champagne, and only one glass, maybe two. And no drinking and driving together, missy!"

She smacked my arm until I let her go, then put more space between us on the couch, her hands on her cheeks as she pouted at me in annoyance.

"I'm not a baby anymore," she said, petulant.

But you'll always be my baby sister," I countered. "Now, move over here and tell me exactly what is going on with Dad."

She didn't get any closer, but she adopted a serious expression as she leaned against the couch, crossing her arms and legs. Her head rested on the back of the couch, and she rolled it to the side so she was facing me.

"There isn't really much I can say."

"Spill! You were the one calling me up telling me how Dad was in such a bad way that I needed to hurry up and get back here. Hell, even Trent came back! That right there is practically a miracle. I thought we'd all be piled up around Dad's bedside, but here we are, talking about why Dad refuses to see us. You have to tell me something. Especially if Trent came back for this."

If she hadn't already mentioned that Dad hadn't seen Trent either, I would have been even more pissed off than I already was.

Exactly what game was Dad playing? It might be true

that he was sick because Emily had no reason to lie to me, but… could Dad be pulling something on us, and we just didn't know? Why else would he call all of us back like that and not agree to see anyone? It didn't fucking make sense.

"I know, it's a shock that he even came back, isn't it?" Emily finally said. "I called Trent personally and he almost didn't take my call. I was surprised when I told him about Dad and he rushed down here. He got here late, but you could tell he'd basically left the office and come straight home. I almost expected you to get here first with how competitive you are. I'm pretty sure he put off work to make the trip."

"I was busy too, you know," I said defensively. "And unlike some people, we aren't all our own bosses, so it's not like I could have put anything off to rush here, I had to get my own business wrapped up."

Emily rolled her eyes. "I know the work you do is for the family business, and that some of it is shady, but come on, Mason. You *really* couldn't put it off, whatever it was that held you back? You only really hurried your way back here because I told you about Trent, right?"

I pursed my lips because I couldn't deny it. Things were a little strained between Dad and me. I resented him for a lot of things, but he was still my dad. My relationship with Trent was just as strained, but I did sometimes make an effort to reach out to my older half-brother. It wasn't that I hated him. His attitude could get annoying, sure, but I was lucky I didn't have to spend much time around him, so it didn't always bother me. He could be as bossy as Dad was, and I avoided that like the plague.

What I really hated was Dad comparing me to Trent. Other than our looks, Trent and I weren't really alike at all. We didn't have the same interests, hobbies, or goals in life, from what I could see. Dad wanted me to be more responsible like Trent, so he made me quit rugby and take a job with the family. I didn't know just how much work Trent did for Dad besides working on his own company, but he made Dad proud in a way my own efforts never seemed to achieve.

The wild partying had begun as a sort of rebellion on my part. Recently, it had grown into something of a routine for me. One that left me drained at times, but one I wasn't willing to just do away with either.

"Is there any reason Dad is refusing to see me?" I asked, looking over to Emily.

She shrugged, not meeting my eyes. "He hasn't really given a definite reason. I haven't seen him myself, not since he came back in an ambulance. Don't worry, though. The moment he agrees to see me, I'll talk him into seeing you guys, too. Kevin is a bit late, but he should be arriving either today or tomorrow. He'll probably get the same treatment…"

She continued to talk, but I wasn't paying attention anymore. Instead, I thought about how odd Dad's actions were. There was no reason for him not to see us unless he was hiding something.

No fucking way, I thought to myself. Is the old man actually pulling a fast one on us?

Was he really ill? Or was it just a ploy to bring us all

home? It was enough to get the prodigal eldest son home, after all.

Not that there was anything I could do about it even if he was. The old man might be a bit of hardass, and this might be a ploy, but he must have done it for reason and I suspected he'd got just what he was after. Now, rather than face the music, he was hiding so we wouldn't know he hadn't been ill at all. I laughed to myself, seeing the plan now. Dad was a wily old man, I'd give him that.

The moment I confirmed Dad was just playing with us, I'd be on the earliest flight out. I cared about my dad, but I'd always hated how he'd tried to control my life as if he had the right to. Anger, amusement, and resentment roiled in my head until it started to pound.

"Let me know how it goes with Dad," I told Emily, rising from the couch. "I'm going to head up to my room now."

I had some hours to spare before my room back at the hotel was fully cleaned. There was a room upstairs that would let me sleep off the night of partying and thoughts about that maid.

5

LAURA

ork was technically over but I was still at the hotel, waiting in the staff lounge for Jessi to have the time to meet me.

She was acting even stranger than usual, and I was really growing more curious about what had happened between her and Trent that changed things so much. Ever since that night, she'd either asked to stay at my place or she'd gone to her parents. Wherever she'd ended up, it wasn't her place, and that was odd for a woman as independent as Jessi.

"Laura!"

I looked up as Jessi finally walked in. She was still dressed in her chef's uniform, which was covered in flour and stains. She wore an expression that said she was beyond exhausted. She did manage to muster up a smile for me though.

"You can go change first," I said, waving a hand at her. "Get changed and come meet me here."

She nodded, changing direction to head for the locker rooms. I'd already changed and was on one of the couches, reading on my phone. Reading was a luxury I didn't allow myself often because it took up time, and I preferred physical books to e-books, but sometimes it was easier than giving into boredom.

With Jessi not far behind, I quickly skimmed over what I was currently reading, bookmarked the page on my browser, and put my phone in my purse. Just in time for Jessi to join me, back in casual clothes, with her purse slung over her shoulder. She dropped into the couch on the opposite side from where I sat, heaving a heavy sigh as her head tilted back and her eyes slid closed.

"You know, Jessi," I said. "You're not supposed to fall asleep in here. You might just spend the night like that, and it's not good for you."

"I do know that," she grumbled, one eye opened in a slit to glare at me. "But I just need to rest for a minute. Today left me so fucking drained…"

I watched her silently with growing concern. Jessi wasn't usually like this. She and I got along so well because she was normally happy and could keep up with the usually perky me. When we hung out, it usually ended with us sitting close together giggling about something, either the latest weird and funny rumors surrounding the hotel, or about guys. I didn't date nearly as much as I'd insinuated to her so many times, and I knew that even though she was past her mid-twenties, she'd never actually dated before.

It was why this whole situation was giving her so much grief and making me worry about her every time I heard the young heir's name. The dread I felt was almost close to when I heard Mason's name, usually as I was called up to fix his room after another wild party. There was plenty to be grateful for on that front, even though he was always annoying when he visited, he didn't spend that much time around Charlotte within the year. I could be sure about Mason leaving.

Jessi didn't have the same assurance with Trent, who happened to be the eldest son and, or so I'd heard, the one to inherit most of the Thompson Empire.

"Hey," I said after a few minutes when she didn't lift her head up. "Are you sure you're okay?"

Feeling a little worried, I put a hand on her forehead. She didn't move to pull it off, but I sat back with a sigh of relief.

"You don't have a fever, but you seriously look like shit. You've worked much longer shifts than today, and usually I find you still energetic at the end of the day. So why is today so different?"

"Because usually I love doing what I do. I enjoy my job, so how could it be draining?"

"What's the problem today?"

She shrugged. "It's nothing, really. I'm just stressing myself too much. I keep getting distracted which leads to making mistakes, which leads to getting reprimanded by the head chef." Suddenly, she sat upright, looking at me with a frown. "Can you believe it? I was scolded! That hasn't happened to me since my first few months working here, and that was years ago."

"You're just going through a rough patch," I said sympathetically, leaning closer to pat her knee and trying to reassure her that not only was I her friend, but her best friend and she didn't need to make me an enemy. After I developed cancer, positive thinking was the only thing that kept me going and I wasn't about to stop now.

"I'm sure you'll get your groove back! After all, not only are you a professional, your creations are world class. If you didn't want to come home so quickly after your studies in France, you could have made a real name for yourself."

The story had been an interesting one to hear. Jessi's family wasn't particularly privileged, the only reason she managed to score a ticket out of the country, was because of her abilities as a pastry chef. I knew she'd worked in France for some time, though she never gave much detail because for most of that time she was simply improving herself, not going out to have fun in the streets of Paris.

If it had been me, I would have had at least a little bit of fun. But that was me.

"You're right," Jessi said, looking at me with a stunned expression like it never occurred to her. "I don't know why I'm letting this get me so badly. I am a professional, and this is my job! I can't keep letting my shit life interfere with my job."

"That's my girl," I said with a wide grin, feeling happy that I'd made her feel better. I scooted closer for a hug that she returned readily. "I know things have been hectic for you since the Thompson boys started flocking home. And I've probably said this enough times for you, but seriously. If you want to talk about anything at all, I'm here for you."

She stiffened a little before she pulled out of my arms. She had this guilty expression on her face. I smirked because I knew she was keeping something from me and ran my hands over her hair in a motherly fashion.

"We've been friends for a while, so I'm letting things slide for now. Just don't stress yourself too much at work, all right? You might collapse in the end, and that would be bad. Stress is bad for your health." I should know, after all. I was all about health for the past several years.

"I guess you're right," she conceded, making me smile.

"Right now, you should get home. Get something nice to eat, take a warm bath, and go to sleep. It'll eat some of the stress of the day away, and I'm going to go home and do the same, okay?"

"Sure," she said, pushing herself off the couch. "Come on, I'll walk you out. Would you like me to drive you back? I came with the car."

"Why, Jessi," I said with a giggle. "How chivalrous of you. Sadly, I can't let you play prince charming for me today. I'm okay with walking home."

"It's dark though," she protested, her eyes flicking to the windows.

"And the streets around here are pretty safe at night," I pointed out. "Not to mention often used and well lit. For tonight, just look after yourself, and I'll look after me, all right? Text me when you get home?"

I held my hand out to her, and even though she rolled her eyes at me, we shook on it.

Feeling the problem had been taken care of, I walked Jessi to her car. It was a slow walk, the cold air waking her up a little, so I wouldn't be worried about her getting behind the wheel.

"Drive slow, okay?" I called after her as she pulled out of the parking lot.

With a smile and a wave out the window, she was gone.

I hummed on my way back home, pulling my scarf and jacket tighter around me to keep out the chill.

I ruffled my bag for the keys as I walked into my building, then made my way up the stairs, jingling my keys, happy to be home. It was a tiny place, small and simple. But for me, even if I was usually alone on the days I didn't bring Jessi home with me, it was all I needed.

I couldn't help but think of Mason and the Thompson family and their grand mansion. I'd heard about how big it was, but I'd never had a reason to get close enough to see it for myself. They had so much, and even a fraction of what they had would have made a difference for when I'd first got sick. If someone had given me that money though, I wouldn't have learned the more important things in life. Like how important it was to give to others and be happy with just a smile in return.

I wondered if Mason knew what the important things in life were. I doubted it. The boy partied all night then walked around naked in front of the help the next morning. It was like he thought we weren't real people or something.

"Whatever," I muttered to myself, dropping my stuff on the couch. "I need to stop bringing work home with me. Especially when it involves that boy."

I shook the thoughts off and went to make myself a

quick dinner. I'd already eaten a bit at the hotel before leaving, so it was just something light. After I was done, it was still too early to go to sleep, so I took my latest knitting project and sat with it on my couch.

Knitting was something I'd picked up over the course of my illness, while I went in and out of the hospital. I'd had plenty of time on my hands, and if I didn't feel like calling up my friends, there were only so many ways to occupy myself. When I'd gone through chemotherapy and gone bald as a result, I'd picked a direction with my knitting. Even now, years later, I still knit hats and head covers for other cancer patients when I had the free time. When I found out I was in remission, I'd wanted to give back to other patients still fighting, and though it wasn't exactly something I would have imagined for myself, it became my way of doing it.

I wonder how Mason would look in one of my hats?

Where had that come from? I saw him naked earlier and now I was thinking of knitting something for him, not getting down and dirty with him. No, ever since I'd lost my breast, the last thing I wanted was for a man to be touching me, knowing that part of me wasn't real. That was until I saw Mason naked in the suite.

Why was I still thinking about him? Even though I'd left work behind, I couldn't get him off my mind! The guy was such an asshole so why did he interest me so much? Though to be honest, I did like looking at his hot body, particularly his tight ass. I could tell he took care of himself, and I hadn't seen a man that fit before. Shit, I was heating up just thinking about it.

"He's gorgeous," I admitted to myself, crossing my arms over my chest. "He is, and he knows it. But being hot means fuck all if he's an ass on top of it."

There was no reply from my empty apartment, but it wasn't like I even needed one. I knew how things had to be between him and me, and for that, I would never put myself on the road to heartbreak by actually wishing for more. I could allow myself to dream about it though because I knew it was going to happen regardless.

That was all it was going to be though. A hot little fantasy for me to take to bed. On that note, I jumped up off my couch, turned off the light in the living room, and rushed to my bedroom as I pulled off my clothes, heading for my cold, empty bed.

6

LAURA

The next morning, I didn't want to get out of my now warm and cozy bed. My mind slowly woke up as I slid off the bed and headed for my bathroom. After a quick shower, I dressed and went to the kitchen to make a light breakfast. I glanced at the knitting I'd left on the couch last night and sighed.

"It's almost time to visit the hospital again, huh…"

The local hospital had a cancer center where I usually dropped my creations off. While I was there I'd go in for a checkup. I was officially cancer free but it was recommended by my doctor to go for regular checkups in case the cancer came back. No one would force me to go, but I did it for the sake of my health.

I put my knitting away in a box back in my bedroom where I already had a few other hats I'd finished. Then I checked the time and cursed, hurrying out of my apartment. I locked my front door, pulled up some music on my phone, threw my bag over my shoulder and headed out with my earphones in. I listened to my usual playlist as I walked to the hotel, letting the music drive my steps.

The trip wasn't exactly a long one, and though there were some bus stops in between where I lived and the hotel, I usually didn't bother taking it, and not just because I'd have to be half an hour earlier. The walk to work was the one time every day where I got to breathe some fresh air. Though just how fresh that air was I wasn't sure as all the cars went by.

When I arrived at the hotel, it was at my usual time, not a little late like yesterday. There were a few people already in when I went to the locker room to change into my uniform, and someone had been nice enough to put on a pot of coffee in the staff lounge, so I got myself a cup. There were some muffins too, and I wondered if they were bought or if Jessi made them. One bite was enough to assure me that she did. My eyes drifted toward the doors to the kitchens, and I thought of going to see her. Then I figured she was fine and let it be. Besides, I had my own work to do.

Just before I could pick up a trolley of supplies and start making my rounds, I was called to a halt.

"Laura, can I talk to you?" Margret Jones asked, and she wasn't just another colleague. She also wasn't really asking because she was the head of the cleaning department, which pretty much meant she was in charge of us maids.

My heart skipped a beat after she called my name because it wasn't usually a good thing when Margaret interrupted our work, since we all had set schedules that detailed where we'd start work from. Occasionally, she'd do inspections of a maid's work or respond to a client's complaints if they said something about the state of their rooms.

So it was with dread that I stopped and slowly turned to face her, waiting to hear what I'd done wrong. Instead of looking her usual prim and haughty self, she looked a little unsettled. Her hair was still put up in that severe bun, and she had on her pristine skirt suit uniform, black with gold trim, with a white blouse and gold scarf tied elegantly at her neck, to match the hotel's colors. Her hands were clasped in front of her, and she kept rubbing them together.

"Is there something I can do for you, Ms. Jones?" I asked, being as polite as possible and hoping she'd called my name by accident.

It was as if she'd drawn a complete blank. I didn't know whether to prompt her again or not, but then her back straightened and she clasped her hands behind her back instead.

"You're not in trouble, Laura," she said quickly, probably reading my awkwardness all over my face. That was something I needed to work on—being so easy to read. "I called you because you have a special assignment today, and you'll be going to do that first."

I held back the groan I wanted to let out. 'Special assignment' couldn't possibly mean anything good.

"What do you mean?" I asked. "Are you sure no one in my block complained or something?"

"Um, no." There was a slight furrow in her brow, and it was enough to alert me. "There were no complaints, but a client did call and ask for you by name, and it's a little far from your usual block. You'll just work there for now, and once you're done you can go on with your usual routine."

The feeling of dread in my chest had solidified. I had the most horrible thought, and looking at Margaret trying to act all nonchalant, I knew it had to be true.

"Was it… Mason Thompson's room, by any chance that called for me?" I asked, and I could hear my voice shake. He wouldn't do that would he? He'd barely even noticed me!

"He did," she admitted. "I don't know why because we sent someone to him already, but he sent her back, then called with your name and description."

I wondered why he'd even call for me, or how he knew my name. Did he ask the maid they'd sent?

"Can I just ask if there was a party or something? Or if he has any guests?" The worry thickened my throat and made it hard to speak.

"Not that I know of. Although, the request came yester-day, and since you were busy, he instructed you be sent as soon as you come in, no need to bother calling first. He insisted on his room being the first you worked on today."

I rolled my eyes at what I knew was a demand from a spoiled little rich boy. I couldn't exactly refuse, so I got some supplies and went on my way after Margaret gave me the room number. It was four floors above where I usually worked, and I sighed, already feeling that today was going to be tiring.

With the thought that Mason would possibly still be in the room, I set out to do my job. I paused outside his door, stalling for a minute, dreaming of just walking away and ignoring the kid's summons, but in the end I sighed and opened the door, unlocking it with my hotel card.

"Dang!" I hissed to myself when I got a look at the room.

It was pretty messed up. There must have been some other people there at some point because there were empty bags of junk food thrown around, and a few bottles of beer here and there. There were spills on the floor—thankfully nothing on any of the rugs—but cleaning it all up would just take time. And it had all been left since yesterday, so it smelled.

The very first thing I did when I went in was to open the window, then pick up the bottles, wrappers, and bags to throw in the trash bin. I'd pack it all up and go with it afterward, but it was best to just leave it for the moment.

Next, I looked through the rest of the suite, freezing when I walked into the bedroom, to find Mason asleep and sprawled over his bed on his stomach, arms folded on his pillow and head on his chest. He had a sheet over him that covered the tops of his thighs, but nothing else. For a moment, I was tempted to just stand there and admire, but then I got a hold of myself. Then, I was furious.

I was summoned to his room as if I was his personal maid and what was he doing? Sleeping as if he didn't have a care in the world. He was a grown man acting like a spoiled little kid and he was living the easy life. I'd had to struggle through life, beating one of the deadliest killers on the planet. Then to make ends meet, I'd had to get this job and be subjected to this? I was better now, physically and financially than I'd been for a few years, but this kid who was younger than me by about a decade had seen more of the world than I even knew existed!

In a moment of weakness, I thought about how unfair it was. I resented the fate that gave so much to some while denying even the bare necessities to others, because I knew there were some that were far worse off than I'd ever been. I didn't let that negativity stay with me for long though, as I once again regained myself.

I knew the world wasn't fair. If it was, I wouldn't have been left orphaned so young and shafted from foster home to foster home until I became legal age. I'd ended up ill and having to fend for myself. If only I'd had the life, the kind of resources, that this kid had. Life would have been so much easier, even with cancer to deal with. Life never worked like that though, and wishes didn't come true if they weren't something you could realistically work for.

That was the life I knew.

There was even more of a mess in the bedroom, I finally noticed, and I picked up more cans and packages, threw them out, and pulled out the vacuum cleaner, plugging it into the socket. I sent a glance at the kid sleeping on the bed and turned it on with a decidedly wicked grin. The noise was immediate and loud, and I let out a small smirk when he popped up. There was some disappointment as he rolled around and his sheet moved with him to cover his crotch.

"What the fuck?" he growled in a sleepy but irritated voice while rubbing his eyes and squinting at me.

"Housekeeping," I chirped, changing the smirk to a bright smile. "I was asked to come in and clean the room, and not to bother asking if there was anyone in already. Sorry to intrude."

"Do you have to fucking vacuum? It's so damn loud." He grimaced, and I wondered if he was hung-over. He must have had quite a few of the bottles of beer I'd found lying around. I changed the settings on the vacuum. It helped for more efficiency and made the vacuum just a little louder.

"Seriously, could you turn that off?" he asked, raising his voice a little and glaring at me.

"I'm sorry." I gave him a simpering smile. I was flashing teeth and hoped the glare was obvious in my gaze. If he was going to summon me up here, then I was going to fucking do my job, and the kid could suck it up.

There was so much I wanted to tell him. He had no idea how lucky he was to be healthy. I wanted to tell him how he was throwing that away by partying and drinking, eating junk food and spending more time sleeping than exercising, no matter how good his body looked. He was wasting his life by doing all this shit, and I would have liked to have the same shot at life that he did, because why did he get it and not me if he was just going to be fucking ungrateful about it?

He was the boss's son though, and a guest at the hotel, so I held my tongue.

"My superior told me you asked me to come in first thing," I said, raising my voice just a little to be heard over the vacuum. "I have other jobs to do so I'm doing this first, just like you wanted."

There was a sneer on his lips, and he looked pretty angry. That put me in a good mood. If he was going to mess with my life I was going to give him as much hell for it as I could. In a moment, the look in his eyes changed. He blinked some more, the glare going out of his eyes as they ran down my body, the growing heat in them making me shiver.

"Laura," he murmured in that deep, growly voice of his, and just the sound of my name on his lips ran a shiver down my spine.

I hadn't even realized I was paying him so much attention, but I caught the looks he was giving me, and I clocked it when he shifted as if he were leaning toward me, like he wanted to pounce on me. That was enough to make me drop the pretense of working entirely. I shut off the vacuum and held up a hand.

"Whoa there, puppy," I said in a voice that brooked no argument, boss's son be damned. "You're a little too young to even be looking at my yard. Only grown-up dogs get to play in it, so stop it with the looks."

His eyebrows shot up, and there was a look of surprise on his face like he hadn't expected those words to come out of my mouth.

Internally, I sneered at him. Did he expect me to throw myself at him like most of the women he met? I wouldn't sleep with him just because he was rich, good-looking, with a good body and well hung. While I wasn't a virgin, I wasn't promiscuous either, and I was very choosy about my partners because of my health. Another reason he could only ever be a fantasy. There was no way I could even consider taking this kid to my bed. I dated before taking men home, where I'd likely end up taking all my clothes off and they could see all my imperfections.

It might have just been me stereotyping him, but I didn't want a guy that would make me feel self-conscious about my body. Or one that might be so irresponsible he'd give me something else to worry about.

"That's good to know," Mason said simply, then slid off the bed, giving me a naughty grin as he did. I turned to look away as the sheet fell. "I'm going to take a shower now, but please, continue. This whole place is a mess."

I wanted to growl at him and ask why he left it that way when someone already came yesterday and he'd sent them away.

"You can go," I said with my back turned to him. "I promise I won't touch your things."

Mason chuckled. The sound was deep and smooth and did funny things to my insides.

"You know," he said. "I might not be a grown-up dog, but maybe all I need is a little puppy training?"

My eyes widened at his words, and I was frozen for a moment as my mouth opened and closed as I gaped like a fish. He just implied he was interested in me, didn't he? And while I didn't usually fall for such proposals, the 'relationship' between Mason and I was already so complicated, and I had way more interest in him than I should have. I didn't know whether to be mad, indignant, or hopeful, and all three options made me a little annoyed.

By the time I could bring myself to turn around, he'd already slipped into the bathroom. On the table were some bills that hadn't been there before. It was a pretty hefty tip, and it left me kind of mad.

Still, I felt pleased. Not so much about the money… although I couldn't be picky, so of course I pocketed it.

Mason was interested in me. He fucking flirted with me! That didn't mean I was suddenly ready to jump him, though the consideration was there.

He was someone to avoid… but he was oh so deliciously tempting, like those expensive chocolates I liked to torture myself with sometimes. I liked to look and torture myself just imagining how it would taste, even though I knew it would be bad for me in the long run, especially if I ate too much, not to mention the price tag.

I tried not to lose sight of myself, but as I picked up the cleaning, there was a smile on my face that wouldn't leave no matter how many times I tried to straighten my expression.

7

MASON

By the time I got back to my room, it was cleaned, and the maid was nowhere to be found. I looked around, even in the front room, but there was no trace she'd ever been there. I had a towel wrapped around my waist, and I sighed at what a waste it was. I'd wanted her to look at me some more because she had the oddest reactions when she saw me naked. Well, not odd entirely. She definitely looked at me as if she wanted me. There was no fucking denying it. It wouldn't take much to get her to play along.

"Next time!" I pulled off the towel as I went back to the bedroom, as if giving her a good eyeful of what she'd get in time.

I looked through my closet for something to wear. I hadn't packed much to begin with, and I'd have to remember to send my clothes down to laundry or I'd have to buy more outfits. There was a store in the hotel lobby where I could buy more clothes if I wanted to, so it wasn't like it was an especially large problem.

"He's going to be mad I'm late," I said aloud, checking the time.

After so much relaxation the past couple days, it was time to get back to work before Trent specifically called me up to ask if I was getting things done. I wondered if Kevin was keeping up with the work since he arrived, or if I was being excessively lazy. Not that Kevin was lazy, he was just as easily distracted as I was, if not more so.

I got dressed in a pair of slacks, then pulled on a white button-down shirt, before grabbing a coat to go over it. Then I put on my loafers and left my room. I could have had some breakfast, but I was allowed to order from the kitchen, and it was easier than just making something myself, or eating whatever junk food I still had in my fridge. I didn't play competitive sports anymore, so I'd gone a bit—well, a lot—lax about my diet. I knew it was self-destructive though, so I usually made sure to have at least one good meal a day.

Besides, the food from the kitchen, particularly the pastries, was pretty amazing stuff.

I made my way to the elevator, then up to what was usually Dad's office, on one of the highest floors in the hotel. The office that Trent was currently using.

Dad's secretary looked up as I neared, and I sent her a nod in greeting.

"Is he busy?" I asked, gesturing toward the door.

"He's looking over some files. You can go in, Mr. Thompson."

I rolled my eyes. "As I've asked before, you can call me Mason. There are too many Thompsons around now, best not to get all confused."

It wasn't the first time I'd asked, but I knew she wouldn't listen to me anyway. She didn't even call my dad by his first name, and she'd been working for him for over half a dozen years.

I opened the door and walked inside. I could have knocked, but I wasn't nearly that polite.

"Busy, as always," I said, closing the door behind me.

Trent was looking over a file on his desk and something on his computer. I didn't know exactly what work he did, but pretty much every time I walked into his office, he was working on something. He was the opposite of me, more work than parties, and even those, I knew he usually ignored unless it wasn't a possibility. Besides working for the family, he'd started up his own successful business and he was only 31.

I was pretty sure some of that success came from the family name, but he definitely worked hard enough I could believe most of it was his being a workaholic. Dad had told me all about big brother's best qualities. And while I resented Dad for comparing us, I didn't particularly hate Trent, or I wouldn't be able to stand being in the same room as him.

"Sorry," he said, not sounding the least bit apologetic. "Dad left a lot of work behind and I've been trying to get through it as quickly as possible, but I've been in between meetings the past few days…"

"You could let Kevin do some of it, or I could handle

some of the meetings, if you wanted," I offered like a fucking chump. Next thing I'll be doing is a fucking curtsey. I was being so accommodating that it was making me feel sick.

He spared me a glance before returning to his computer.

"As much as I appreciate that, I'm fine doing this much. I only need to keep it up until Dad is ready to come back…"

His words trailed off, and I noticed when his eyes glazed over. He was no longer focusing on what was on his computer, and I wondered if he had the same thoughts I did about how odd this whole thing with Dad was.

"Have you had any word yet?" I asked.

He looked up at me, a slight frown on his brow. "If you're asking about Dad, still nothing. I'm too busy to push it for now. I'll give it another week or so, then go back to the mansion."

"You went there?" I asked.

His lips pursed. "The day I arrived, yes. I've been staying at the hotel ever since."

I nodded because it was completely expected. It was a surprise he'd even stepped foot there, considering he hadn't since he left for college. I went back occasionally to see my parents and my sister, and so did Kevin. Then I remembered Emily had mentioned something about him arriving before I did. I was partying way too hard if I'd forgotten that little nugget.

"Can I help you with something?" he asked, folding his arms on the desk and giving me his full attention.

I shrugged. "I came to see whatever else needs doing around here. I'm done with the last task, so I was thinking of making some rounds in the departments…"

He nodded slowly, considering.

"That would be useful, actually. I haven't had the chance to get out of this office much if it isn't for some meeting. Make the rounds. I'll be getting some reports from the departments and you can help me assess them."

"Sure," I said, turning around to leave. "I'll get to that now. I'll send some quick reports tonight and we can talk tomorrow."

"Good luck," he called as I left, and I could hear he was already getting distracted with his own work.

The floor I was on only held the executive offices. Other offices were on the lower floors, and I made my way down to the closest one. As I was passing through the hallway, a maid walked past me, and that was all it took to bring back the image of that maid from earlier.

Laura. I'd asked the woman they'd sent yesterday—who'd been more than ready to throw herself at me, even though I'd turned her down—about the other maid. She'd told me her name was Laura, though I didn't get a second name or much information about her besides she was a generally happy person. Not that I'd seen that particularly.

A smirk crossed my lips as I thought of how she'd looked at me this morning. She'd been smiling of course, but I hadn't missed the hostility in her gaze, like I'd personally offended her. And even then, she'd been looking at me, checking me out the entire time. I almost got the idea she resented me for being so good looking.

She was so fucking fun to tease, which is why I'd tried to be fast with my showering, just so I could see her reaction to seeing me in nothing but a towel and still wet at that. She did her work pretty fast though. Not that I'd messed up my suite so badly after a group of maids had cleaned after my latest party. I'd only had a small gathering with some of my friends who'd hung around after the party, though they'd probably be leaving soon. Just as well, because I had work to do.

So far, no one had reported my partying to Trent, and I only knew that because I knew he'd complain if he'd actually heard something.

Laura, though… it wasn't usual for me to get someone so stuck in my mind, but I had to admit she was interesting. She was spunky, and as much as she played at being polite, I knew she wasn't the kind of woman who'd take my shit. Every time I saw her, she was seemed to be looking at me with irritated eyes, with just a hint of interest that told me she at least found me attractive. She'd been looking around at the mess I made with disdain and resignation. Every time I saw her expressions, before she tried to hide them, I was left smiling.

Her body doesn't hurt, either.

She wasn't like one of the skinny girls that usually made a play for me. She had some delicious curves I couldn't help but want to lay my hands on, and she wasn't throwing herself at me for my looks, or my money and connections, so she was a challenge.

"I can't touch her," I muttered, a frown replacing the smirk on my lips.

In spite of my attraction to her, she was still a maid at my dad's hotel. It would be so fucking hypocritical of me to try to do more than tease her, when it was me who kept warning Emily against fraternizing with the help. She was just making friends with them. I wanted to take this woman to my bed and keep her there for a while. It was always me who cautioned her about being friends with them, because it was bad for keeping up her image, and the family image. I couldn't just eat my own words and pursue this woman.

How long would I be able to hold out though? The more I got to know about Laura, even if it was only in bits and pieces in our short, impersonal encounters, it only fueled my desire for more. As odd as it felt, I was really growing to like her, considering my eyes always looked toward her, and I had no idea when I'd even started doing it. I just realized one day, that when I had my room cleaned and she was among the maids doing the cleaning, my gaze always found her.

I knew she was a bit older than me, but age was just a number, right?

8

MASON

Things were getting busy, and it was a while before I stopped and realized it had been more than a week since my last party, or for that matter, any sort of fun.

"Hey, Mason!"

I looked over my shoulder to see Kevin running down the hall to me. I sighed and walked the few steps to the elevator and pressed the button for one going up. Then I turned around and waited for my little brother to catch up.

"What's up? I'm surprised to see you here," I said trying to be friendly, but it didn't work, because I knew that with Kevin I was wasting my breath.

"We've both been working here," he pointed out.

Sure, why the hell was I so distracted?

He came to a stop beside me, grinning. "I'm done with all the stuff I was supposed to do outside of the hotel. What about you?"

"I have a few reports I'm taking up to Trent," I said,

holding up a folder to show him. "After this, I'm going to have a quick little vacation before he finds more work for us to do."

The elevator opened before he could say something in response. The few people inside walked out, so it was just the two of us as we got inside the elevator.

"There's still no word on Dad," he said, leaning against the wall. "I tried talking to Emily and Mom, and neither of them had anything to say. Mom was acting weird and Emily kept changing the subject."

I narrowed my eyes, suspicions about Dad renewed. I didn't share any of them with Kevin though. He probably had some of his own ideas anyway. I pushed those thoughts to the side as the elevator came to a stop and the doors opened on my floor. I walked out with Kevin, and we both headed for the office.

Half an hour later, I was walking out of the office, leaving Trent to deal with Kevin. My stomach growled as I got back into the elevator, and I ran a hand over it, realizing I hadn't eaten the whole day. I figured I'd just go down to my room and order room service, but as I went to push the button for my floor, another thought occurred to me. One that made me smirk.

It had been some time since I'd seen Laura. I hadn't forced her to come to my place to pick up after me again. Since I was seriously working, I didn't even get to see the maid that did clean my place anymore, not that I made much of a mess when I spent most of the day out of the room.

So instead of pressing the floor to my room, I pressed

for the lobby, checking the time on my watch. It should be late enough that most of the staff were packing up to go home, leaving the staff on the night shift.

I got out and headed straight for the staff area. I hadn't been there in quite some time, but I always knew where it was because there had been plenty of complaints about me sent to my father, particularly the cleaning staff.

I ducked into the room without bothering to knock, and at first, I didn't think there was anyone in there, though the light was on in the room. After a moment of listening, I heard a sniffle and paused before retreating from the doorway. I was torn for a moment, wondering if I should interfere or not, but then took a step inside.

"Hello?" I called, so whoever it was wouldn't get spooked.

I'd walked in this place enough times to know the layout. The front was a lounge room with several seats and tables around the room, with a few plants, framed pictures, and knickknacks to brighten up the space. There were doors that led to the lockers where the staff stored their uniforms. Doors that led to the main kitchens, and an open arch that led to the kitchen used by the staff for their meals. I'd found it ridiculous that they had separate kitchens, but I wasn't about to tell Dad how to run his business.

The sniffling was coming from in there, and when I followed the sound, I found just the person I wanted to see in the last state I expected to see her in.

"Laura?" I said. "Are you crying?"

She must not have heard my call from before because

when she looked up at me, there was shock in her expression. There were also tear tracks on her cheeks, and she wiped them away quickly with another sniff.

"Sorry," she said quickly, her voice thick. "Um, it's just the onions. I figured I might as well make something to eat before I head home. Some of the guys coming in for the night shift aren't the best at cooking, and usually food is left for them but everyone ate it all today."

I wanted to point out that I hadn't asked for an explanation, but she probably didn't need me to be snarky at that moment. Instead, I looked at the counter in front of her, then arched an eyebrow.

"You know, that would have been a good excuse if you'd cut any onions," I said motioning to the vegetables she'd cut up. There wasn't an onion in sight. "Unless you want to tell me the carrot made you tear up. Maybe the cucumber?"

She blinked at me, then looked down at the counter. When she looked back up there was a trembling smile on her lips as she let out a small huff.

"If you knew it was just an excuse, you could have let me off."

I shrugged. "I'm not the kind of guy that does that."

She sighed, though the sound almost sounded fond. "No, I guess you wouldn't be Mason Thompson if you did. You're too fucking tenacious for your own damn good. Or so the stories go, unless it had to do with your dad."

I let out a sigh myself as I moved closer to lean back against the counter. "There's no point in going against Daddy dearest. He claims to only want the best for us, and children are meant to be obedient, no?"

At that, she gave me a wry look, before she went back to cutting vegetables. While she did it with ease, it wasn't as fast as I'd seen Emily work the few times she'd forced me to sit down to one of her meals.

"Can I ask what is making you cry? If it's something no one should know, I promise to keep it a secret."

"It's nothing," she said dismissively.

"It can't be nothing," I said insistently. "Not if it's making you cry alone. If you're hesitating because it's me, just think of me as some random person and tell me. I'm a pretty good listener."

She snorted, though I couldn't know if it was because she didn't want to spill her troubles to a random person or me of all people. Maybe it was a reaction to me calling myself a good listener. There were more sides to me than just being a partying playboy, and I hoped she'd stick around long enough to see that.

"It's… my friend," she said haltingly. "She, um… she worked here with me, as one of the chefs in the kitchen. I'm just a little sad because she moved. It was sudden, and I know she's in pain wherever she is, but I can't do a thing to help her."

"Why did she move?" I asked, frowning.

She stopped her cutting to stare up at me, the look searching. I tilted my head in a silent question.

"My friend, you see," she started, keeping her eyes on me. "She has this man she likes. Well, more like, has been in love with for years, only this man never gave her a second glance or a kind word. Until recently anyway, and she didn't outright tell me but I guess that they had an affair.

But the man was someone important, someone powerful, and he'd broken her heart before. So she left before he could have the chance to break it once again."

I arched an eyebrow in the middle of her story, wondering if she was telling me the plot of some romance novel. But she'd obviously taken this seriously, so I decided to do the same. Then I frowned, wondering… there was no fucking way it could be my dad, right? It would be nothing like him, but I'd no problem picturing him in a whirlwind romance with a younger woman. From what I knew, it hadn't been long after Trent's mom's death when he suddenly married my mom and had the three of us.

Although it would certainly explain the sudden heart attack and him refusing to see us, no matter how many times we tried. But I shook that off with a chuckle. Even if there was a grain of truth in it, it was a worry for another time. Instead, I focused on the beautiful woman still crying and sniffling in front of me. She looked like she needed a friend. I was right there, so why not volunteer?

"What exactly are you making?" I asked, stepping forward. I'd taken off my coat sometime during the day, and I undid my cufflinks, put them in my pocket, and then rolled back my shirt sleeves.

She glanced at me curiously. "Why do you want to know?"

I shrugged. "You've cut up so much; I'm not quite sure what it is you're trying to make. If you'd like dinner, I could help you cook. As long as I get to eat some because I'm pretty hungry myself."

As if to agree with me, my stomach grumbled. Her

mouth was open, probably to complain, but at the sound, she closed it. She didn't give any verbal confirmation, but she did step a little to the side, giving me space on the counter.

"You know how to cook?" she asked, as I looked around for ingredients.

"Sure. I'm a bachelor and I live on my own. There's a kitchenette in my suite, and I have stuff in my fridge. I'm pretty good at handling my meals."

Whatever she was going with, cutting up so many vegetables, I looked through the fridge and decided on steak. We worked with each other, as she made her dish and I made mine. Pretty soon, the wafting scent filled the kitchen, and I could feel my stomach grumble some more.

Once the food was done, I set the table in the kitchen, big enough for about ten people, though I figured some of them would eat in the lounge area instead. It didn't matter as long as they cleaned everything up later. Laura set down her dishes of baked potatoes and steamed vegetables.

"We have a wine selection," she told me, pointing me in the right direction. "You'd be a better pick than me. Just know we can't have too much or I'd have to replace the entire bottle."

I went to where she'd pointed. The selection was pretty shallow, but I managed to find a decent red I recognized as a good brand, even though I was more of a beer kind of person. I found a corkscrew and opened it.

"Dinner is served," I muttered as I rejoined her at the table, setting down the wine and glasses.

I poured some wine into both glasses, then we both dug in.

"So," I started, cutting a bite-sized piece of the steak and popping it in my mouth. "Why don't you tell me a bit about yourself?"

She hummed. "Where do I start?"

"I don't care. When you were a kid, your family, friends, where you grew up…"

"That's a lot of questions," she noted dryly but didn't complain. "So, family… I guess I don't have any. I lost my parents when I was young, Dad first, then Mom later on. I didn't know until way later it was because my mom was sick. I think Dad just had an accident. I believe I have some relatives… but none of them stepped up to look after me before, so I went into the foster system."

"And how did that work out for you?"

She sighed. "Not too bad, not too great. I was moved to a few homes, and I met a lot of good people. It's just that… in the end, I remained alone. I made friends of my own in college, but then I moved. Oh, and I grew up in the mountains of North Carolina, and lived over there until about ten years ago." She arched her eyebrows at me. "Is that enough for you?"

I shook my head, taking a sip of wine then waving a hand at her. "Not at all. Please, tell me more."

So, we ate, and we talked, and drank wine. Laura forgot her sadness, and I even got to see her laugh, surprising myself when I ended up laughing as well in some moments. Even after we finished eating, we poured another glass and talked as we drank in small sips.

When she finished her second glass, I held up the bottle, ready to pour her more, though my glass had been empty for a while. She held a hand up before I could pour it for her.

"I think I've had enough to drink for now," she said. "Thank you, though."

"Oh," I murmured, feeling a little disappointed that our time had come to an end.

I stared at her, waiting for her move to get up to leave before I followed. When she moved to get up, only to freeze, I frowned in confusion. I didn't get the chance to ask what the matter was though, as I watched her expression harden into one of determination like she'd decided something.

"I need to be getting home," she said.

"Want me to drive you home?"

She took in a shaky breath, though her eyes were steady as they met my gaze. "I would love that... and a little more. Would you like to come back to my place with me?"

My eyes widened at the sudden invitation, leaving me floored but interested.

9

LAURA

The question was out of my mouth before I could call it back. Mason was obviously shocked about my proposition, and it was a bit of a struggle not to hide my own surprise.

What did he just say?

"Are you asking me… what I think you're asking me?" Mason asked again after a moment, his voice hesitant.

Right there! That was my chance to clear things up. I opened my mouth to tell him I just wanted the ride and nothing more. That was the path of least regret for the future, I could feel it. And yet, different words left my mouth instead.

"Well, what do you think I'm asking?" I retorted, teasing, but with underlying unease.

What the fuck am I doing! It hasn't been that long since I declared I wouldn't do anything with him because he was out of my league! Two weeks maybe? And with all the shit with Jessi…

This was all probably a bad idea. Letting him see me cry and not sending him off right afterward was where my mistake began. I hadn't seen him in a while, though the fantasies had held, and then to see him in the flesh... it must have been too much for me. Especially with seeing him acting like how I pictured him in some of my fantasies... an attentive man, good enough at holding a meaningful conversation. He was right. He was a pretty good listener.

However, none of that changed anything.

Mason didn't look like he was going to back down as he stood up with sudden enthusiasm, a grin on his face as he held a hand out to me. I stared at the hand, trying to hold myself back.

Then, I had a sudden thought... why not?

Why was I fighting myself so hard, when I had to admit I'd been tempted to get myself off to the thought of this guy and the size of his cock? It had been so long since I'd last been in a relationship, I was almost desperate enough just to jump him and get this over with. He'd only shown minimal interest in me before, so this was my chance, right? He wasn't just laughing his head off at this older woman that lusted after him.

After a moment of staring at his hand, I reached out my own because I had to admit if only to myself that I wanted this, wanted him. There was no shame in it. I placed my palm on his, and his long, rough fingers folded over my hands. My heart thumped hard.

"Would you mind coming back to my room with me?" |he asked, holding my hand.

I blinked at him, my body already heating up at the thought of the two of us getting hot and heavy.

"Huh?"

He chuckled, grinning at me. "I was thinking we could just head up to my room, instead of me taking you home. Would that be inconvenient for you?"

I bit down on my lip. I would have felt more comfortable at my place, but I figured I wasn't going to be thinking much about comfort while trying to get into his pants. Besides, my place was small, and while clean, it wasn't exactly pretty to look at. Then I looked Mason over and decided my bed wouldn't be big enough for the two of us with his six-foot-four frame, especially considering the luxury he was used to.

"Let's do that," I said decisively, getting up.

I pulled my hand out of his to clear the table and wash the dishes we'd used. I already had the rest of the food I'd cooked put away, but where the others could find it when they finally made it in to eat. I was just glad no one had come in to interrupt and found me with Mason, or there would have been rumors all over the hotel about it, and that was the last thing I needed.

With everything done, Mason held his hand out to me, and again, I took it.

He dragged me out into the hall, then to the elevator. Thankfully, he knew where the elevators used by the staff were, so I didn't have to put up with him dragging me through the lobby, in front of guests and other staff.

In the elevator, we stood facing forward, both of us silent. It was a little awkward for me because we were still holding hands. It was hard to stand still, my body was feeling way more than interested, and I couldn't help fidgeting in impatience as I watched the floor numbers go up.

"I never realized how high my room was," Mason muttered.

If he was trying to be witty or something, the joke fell flat. The elevator doors finally opened, and Mason was tugging me out. He let go of my hand again when we stopped in front of his room, so he could find the keycard to unlock the door, then pulled me inside. Out of nowhere, he whirled me around, his other hand going to my shoulder as he held me against the door, and I gasped, my eyes widening as I looked up at him.

"What the—"

He cut me off before I could voice a complaint, his lips slanting against mine in a kiss. I made a noise of surprise, but it only took a second before I was kissing him back. I pulled my hands away from his to place them on his chest, running them up and around his shoulders to wrap my arms around his neck. I leaned up on the tips of my toes, pressing my lips harder against his.

I was getting short of breath, and as I was thinking about pulling back, he broke the kiss first. I was left panting, though Mason seemed to be faring better than I was.

"Damn, Laura," he muttered, huffing a small laugh.

My face felt a little hot. "Sorry. It's been a while for me."

"Oh?" His eyebrows shot up. "How long is a while?"

I opened my mouth to reply but realized I didn't have a ready answer. How long had it been anyway? More than a year, maybe? I remember getting dumped a long while before last Christmas, and the year was getting on, so nearly.

"A while," I said. No need to go into detail.

He didn't press for more, instead he leaned down for another kiss that I melted right into. After a long, passionate kiss that left my body yearning towards his, I pressed my hands to his chest so he'd let me breathe again.

"Are we ever going to move away from the door?" I asked breathlessly.

Mason grinned at me, then pulled away. He took my hand again and pulled me further into the room. He pulled me over to the couch, directed me to sit down, then sat right next to me, body shifted to the side a little, so he was facing me.

I didn't fight it when he went in for another kiss. We'd already had dinner and conversation. Right then, I only wanted the one thing from him, and as he was pushing me back into the arm of the couch and lying his athletic body over mine, I was all for it. I reacted with enthusiasm, in fact, throwing one of my legs over his, my fingers burying in his hair to hold him to me as I kissed him back with as much passion as he was giving me.

He nibbled on my lower lip, making me moan. His tongue slid into my mouth, tangling around mine, and I sucked on it. Mason let out a growl that ran a shiver down my back, pressing me further into the couch. When he pulled away again, I was lying down on my back, my legs thrown over his, and he was half kneeling on the couch with his upper body braced above me, one hand on the arm of the couch.

Mason didn't slow down, moving to kiss his way down my neck. His other hand went to my waist, flexing a little as he slowly, seductively moved it up.

That was where I got scared, and I put a hand over his to stop him. It was enough to get him to freeze completely. He slowly pulled back to meet my eyes, his own full of questions. Suddenly feeling awkward again, I looked away from his gaze.

"What is it?" he asked, his voice in a whisper.

I sighed, pushing against his chest some more. He moved until he was sitting properly, and I shifted my legs from over his to do the same. I fixed my slightly mussed clothes, my hands on my knees.

"Did I do something wrong?" he asked quietly, after a minute of silence.

"No, you didn't do anything wrong. It's just that... I don't usually do this sort of thing."

"Having sex?" he responded, his tone incredulous.

I let out a snort at that. "No, not that. I'm not a virgin, Mason. I just... don't do one-night stands. Usually, I date guys before I sleep with them. I want to do this though," I added quickly, so he didn't think I was asking him to date me. "It's just..."

As I went to explain, my voice trailed off. Usually, I dated guys to gauge their reactions to when we both wanted something more out of the relationship. It had taken a while for me to grow comfortable with my body the way it was because while my scars were a mark I would have to live with for the rest of my life, they were also a mark that I'd escaped death once, so it was a big thing.

Still, I wasn't so comfortable that I would let just anyone look at me so exposed. I might have got my life back on track; I was able to carry on happily like I hadn't had a bad experience in my life. That didn't mean I would be okay with people judging my body, and it was why I didn't date that much. I was in my mid-thirties, and I'd dated maybe five guys, and one of them was before the whole cancer thing. Of the remaining four, only three ever made it to my bed. One of those relationships lasted over a year, but we still broke up. He was the guy who'd left me last year because he'd fallen for someone else.

I could be fine with everything else in my life, but over this, I couldn't be so carefree. I didn't like that I was so self-conscious because it was something I hadn't had before, but it wasn't something about me that I could easily change either.

"There's something you should know…"

Mason arched an eyebrow at me. He didn't dismiss me though. He sat back and crossed his arms over his chest.

"Go ahead, Laura. I'm all ears."

10

LAURA

Mason was waiting to hear what I had to say, and at that moment, I hesitated again. I wanted this or I wouldn't have taken the guy's hand in the first place, so I took in a deep breath for courage and decided to spill everything.

"So, this thing you should know… it might weird you out a little bit," I said in warning, already bracing myself in case he suddenly didn't want to continue.

He shrugged. "It's fine. Just tell me before I jump you."

I sucked in a sharp breath, eyes widening on him. But then I shook my head, determined not to let him distract me.

"Okay, so I was sick a while back, and I needed to have surgery on my chest. One of my breasts was reconstructed and the other one, well, sort of 'lifted'. I also have only one nipple."

The words flowed out of my mouth because I didn't see

much reason in keeping it a secret, anyway. Then I held my breath and waited for his reaction.

He didn't have much of one. He just blinked at me, arched an eyebrow, and his eyes dropped to my chest. The look in them was almost curious.

"If you were worried that would bother me, don't," he said blankly. "I've wanted you for a while now. Since the last time I saw you, I've had you in my head. It's not going to be easy to turn me away."

My jaw dropped a little at his declaration. It wasn't exactly what I expected, but it was a good enough outcome that my nerves quieted a bit. He stood up and held his hand out to me. Once again, I took his hand, and he pulled me up from the couch, then led me over to the bedroom. Then he whirled on me, putting his arms around my waist to tug my body closer to his, and leaned down for another kiss.

Only, it was different from before. There was still passion, but the kiss was softer, almost tender, and as much as I'd loved the rough kissing, this made me melt. This time when his hands lifted my thick top, I didn't stop him. Our lips separated long enough for me to raise my arms so he could pull it off. Mason backed me up slowly until the back of my knees hit the bed, and I fell back onto it, with him following me down, pressing me into the soft, wide mattress. I moaned a little at the luxury. It was like lying down on a fucking cloud.

"Move up," Mason said against my lips.

I let out a groan but did as he wanted. I toed off my shoes, then rose up on my elbows and pushed my way up the bed. Mason followed me, crawling up, so he remained above me, keeping our lips locked. When I lay back down with my head on top of the pillow, he was braced over me on all fours. His eyes, when he pulled back long enough for me to see them, were smoldering.

"Do you have condoms?" I asked before we could go any further. Those were a must with any guy I slept with for the first time.

Mason smirked. He rolled off me to reach for the night-stand, and I pouted a little that he'd moved away. I looked down at my body and let out a shaky breath. I still had on another top and my bra, but already I was feeling exposed. Mason didn't give me long to ponder on it before he was back, settling his body above mine. He held a strip of four condoms up so I could see them before he set them to the side on the bed.

"I hope you don't think we're using all of those," I said, breathless.

Mason just hummed and leaned down to leave a peck on my lips. "Not all of them, no. But more than one at least."

I arched an eyebrow. "You can last for two rounds?" I asked.

He smirked, then leaned down to kiss me some more.

I flinched a little when his hand dropped to my waist. The top I had on underneath was light, and I could feel his hot touch through the fabric. It had been so long since I'd had such large, rough hands on my body. I shuddered when that hand slipped under my top to touch my bare skin, sighing into his mouth as my body squirmed under his. He slid his knee between mine, and I parted my thighs, spreading my legs so he could lower his hips to the space between them. He still had on his slacks, and I was wearing jeans, but even through them, I could feel the hardness of his thighs, and I clamped my legs around him, wanting to feel more of it.

It had been a while for me.

Mason moved from kissing my lips to leaving little kisses all over my face. I had my eyes squeezed shut, and I let out a little giggle when I felt his lips on my forehead, temples, cheeks, and chin. He kissed his way down my jaw, nipping slightly when he got to the flesh of my neck. He nibbled lightly on my ear, which made me gasp. My back arched slightly as a throbbing began between my thighs.

"Fuck, you're good at this," I said in a light growl as he nipped and licked his way down my neck.

His teeth dug in a little at one point as he sucked, and I imagined he'd leave some marks for me to enjoy tomorrow. I'd have to explain them but I'd probably be more smug than embarrassed—as long as I didn't get to see any guests, that is.

"I'd like to think I know how to treat a woman," was Mason's response. "Don't worry about a thing, Laura. Just lie back and enjoy it."

I wanted to protest a little. I wasn't a passive kind of girl, especially not in bed, but Mason was working some magic on me, going to the other side of my neck and repeating the process going down. His tongue dipped in the hollow of my throat, and my head tilted back as I let out a light gasp, my thighs flexing around his.

"So good," I breathed out.

Mason chuckled.

His hand, still on my waist under my top, pushed the light fabric up. My breath hitched, and like he could feel my unease, Mason bit down on the side of my neck, just where it met my shoulder, sucking a little harder. It was enough to distract me, so he had the top up and over my chest before I realized he'd moved it. I helped take it off after a second of hesitation.

He stopped and pulled back, rising on his elbows to look down at me.

"It's your call how far we go tonight," he said, his voice clear, eyes soft as they met mine. "You can keep your bra on if you want."

I didn't want that. Even if he was saying it for my benefit, it would be uncomfortable for me. Sex was messy and sweaty, and having clothes on when I fucked, especially my bra, just felt disgusting afterward.

"It's fine," I said. I arched my back a little and reached behind my back.

Mason didn't try to help as I searched for the clasp of my bra to undo it, and I was grateful. Once I had the clasp undone, I settled back down, crossing my arms over my chest to hold onto the bra straps. I held that pose for a second, taking a deep breath, then slid it off and tossed it to the side.

My eyes wanted to look anywhere but at Mason. Still, I wanted to see the expression on his face, and when my eyes turned away for a moment, they flitted right back.

Mason didn't even seem to hesitate. He leaned down to continue kissing me, starting from my neck and making his way down to my chest. He squirmed a little lower, so his face was level with my chest, his hands cupping both my breasts, squeezing lightly. His lips dropped little kisses all over my breasts, not leaving out my nipples, real and tattooed.

I was thrilled and so fucking happy, feeling shameless as I wrapped my limbs around him, wanting his body as close to mine as possible. His actions were enough to make me give in, and when he wrapped his lips around my nipple and sucked, I let out a little cry as my back arched, pushing my breast even further into his mouth.

"Naked," I gasped, my thighs flexing around his once more as the throbbing between my thighs grew unbearable. "Please, Mason! Clothes off."

He didn't argue, letting out a little groan as he moved, so he was on his knees above me. I moaned a little because I had to pull my legs from around him, but his hand fumbling the button of my jeans was enough to distract me. I did the same, my hands moving to the waistband of his slacks, then around so I could undo his belt, then his button and zip. I tugged his slacks down, and they slid smoothly down his thighs. My jeans were a little too tight for that, and he pulled away to take them off, making me groan in protest.

Mason pulled my jeans lower off my legs as he slid down my body. He tossed them to the side, then did the same for his slacks, pausing for a second before he pulled off his briefs, too. I sucked in a harsh breath, seeing him erect for the first time.

"It's not anything you haven't seen before," he

murmured, crawling back over me, settling his hips between my spread thighs once more.

My eyes stayed on his cock the entire time. Fuck, he was at least ten inches, thick, the head already a flushed pink. Far from being daunted, I wanted him in me, fast. He didn't seem to be in much of a hurry, and he let out a moan as he rocked against me, rubbing his cock against my sex through my panties.

"Don't fucking tease me," I growled, though I ruined the effect when he rocked his hips again and I let out another moan, deeper, throatier.

"I want this to last as long as possible," he said, pressing a kiss to the side of my neck where he'd dug in his teeth before.

Letting out a growl, I ran my hands over his back, sliding down over his ass to cup his cheeks, then another moan as my hands flexed.

"I've dreamed of this ass," I admitted, a little breathless as I squeezed his hard, toned globes in my palms. This time, when he rocked his hips against mine, I shifted my hips up to meet him, letting out a loud cry when the head of his cock rubbed against my clit. I squirmed against him, letting out more cries, feeling like I was close to orgasm already, and he wasn't even in me yet.

Mason let out a husky little laugh that wasn't helping the state my body was in. At last he moved, pulling back to tug off my panties, then reaching for the condoms. My hands got to them first, and I grinned up at him as I tore one from the strip and undid the wrapper. I wrapped my legs around his hips, tugging him lower as I reached between us, and smoothed the condom over his dick. I bit down on my lip, stroking him a few times so I could feel his thick length in my fingers.

He shifted his hips with a hiss, and it was my turn to grin. I was going insane with lust as it was. There was no way I going to hold out just to torture him a little. If we ever did this again, I could try it then. I guided the head of his cock to my entrance, then held my breath as he moved, slowly filling me up. I looked up, and our gazes held as he filled me to the hilt, then froze.

"Move," I whispered, half urgent half pleading.

He didn't wait for me to tell him twice. His hips started a gentle rhythm that had his cock rubbing my insides in all the right spots, ones that made my hips dance and my thighs tense. My hands moved back to his ass, and I moved my hips against him, my nails digging into his ass, trying to get him to move faster.

"Fuck me properly," I moaned against his throat, my tongue nipping out to lick sweat from his silky skin.

"Oh, but I am," Mason purred, ducking his head to place kisses all over my chest. "Don't be so impatient, Laura."

The way my name rolled off his tongue had another shiver running through my body. He didn't make me wait for long, his thrusts becoming deeper, moving faster until he was fucking me hard and deep. I cried out with every thrust, loving the feel of his cock moving in and out of me, feeling so filled by him. My eyes squeezed closed as he fucked me, giving into the sensations pouring all over my body. Little shocks ran through my body, starting from every point where we were connected.

My cries grew louder the closer I got to climax, the pleasure climbing and climbing until I wondered just how high I would go. And then, before I was ready for it, the pleasure burst, and I let out a whimpering moan as my body shuddered, convulsing around Mason's cock, still moving in and out of me. He buried his face in my neck, groaning, as his own body went still, then his hips jerked, his cock throbbing inside of me as he came.

We were both left spent, and he just barely managed to roll us over, so he didn't fall on me and crush me, with his arms going around me and one of my legs thrown over his thighs. I felt drowsy as we caught our breath, and a small smile crept onto my face.

In the next moment, reality kicked in.

The sex was amazing. It made me feel so alive, like I hadn't felt in ages, and I knew I wouldn't regret my decision to sleep with Mason. I also knew that still, nothing would happen between us, because he was still out of my league, and it wasn't like I was the first woman he'd ever taken to his bed. I couldn't help but feel sad about it.

Well, I thought to myself, trying to find some silver lining, at least after this… his room shouldn't be too hard to clean tomorrow.

Unless he decided to have a party or something.

"Should I leave…?" I murmured after some moments, a little unsure how we were going to go about this.

I'd never had a one-night stand or a fling before. I didn't have the time or the chance to before I'd got sick, or the inclination afterward, so the only rules I knew were what I read of in romance novels.

Mason grumbled, his arms around me holding me tighter against his chest. His softening cock slid out of me as we shifted, and I let out a gasp at the feeling. Mason grumbled some more, reaching between us to pull off the condom, then dropping it off the side of the bed, before tugging me close once more. He reached for the sheets and wrapped it around us.

"Would it be a problem if you stayed?" he asked, his voice drowsy.

"I don't have any clothes here…"

"Wear what you had today, then," he said.

I wrinkled my nose. It would be more likely that I woke up to rush home for a change of clothes or something. He didn't seem to want to release me, and I didn't want him to let me go. This little fling would end at some point, but a night of comfort, sleeping in his arms, might not be too bad to indulge in.

11

MASON

I woke up feeling like I was on top of the fucking world. I had a fucking dirty grin on my face and nothing could erase it. Not even Dad and his fucking antics. It lasted for all of two seconds as I stretched across the bed and found it empty.

What the fuck?

I thought I was dreaming, so I looked around and sure enough, the room was empty. Shit, why did she creep out like that? I was thinking about it when I remembered last night and thought, it doesn't matter. Last night was fucking....

Hmm, I couldn't believe that I was lost for words. Me. Mason Thompson. Then I remembered she had to work and that must be why she got up and didn't want to disturb me. I slid out of bed, humming a little tune, and headed for the bathroom to take a shower. No longer feeling dejected, but more like the fucking king of the castle.

I'd see Laura again, there was no doubt about that in my mind. I wasn't sure what had changed yesterday when I'd held my hand out to her. Before she probably would have just turned me down. I felt a little guilty when I thought I used her vulnerability yesterday, just a little bit, to get what I wanted. The decision had ultimately been hers, and she'd had plenty of times to try to back out of it, only she hadn't.

I jumped out of the shower like a rabbit out of a magic hat, toweled myself dry and walked back to the bedroom, and headed for the closet. My mood was put to a dramatic end once again as I thought about going to look for Laura and then remembering that I had to work too. I couldn't start neglecting work, not for any reason. I found another pair of slacks and a shirt, a belt, cuffs, and a coat. I got dressed, then put on a pair of socks and my shoes. I stopped in front of the full-length mirror behind the closet door and grinned at my reflection.

I went to the bed where I opened a drawer on the nightstand. I pulled out a watch and wrapped it around my wrist.

I left my room with my hands in my pants pockets, still humming the same tune under my breath. There was a large smile on my face, but no one there to see it. By the time I got to the elevator and pressed for the right floor, I'd controlled my expression just a little. I was going up to see my brother after all. I didn't want to confuse him, and I didn't want him getting the wrong idea either.

I got off on the right floor and walked down the hall, nodding to the secretary before walking right into the office. Trent was already there, already working, as usual. He had his head buried in his monitor already, scanning reports.

"Do you ever fucking sleep? Or are you living here these days?" There was a jaunty tone to my voice as I broke the silence.

He glanced up from the computer. "Well, I'm always busy. I get off late and I start early, most work is like that. It won't go away if I take extra time to sleep. How's your work been? Anything to do today?"

I crossed the room to sit on the chair in front of his desk, crossing my legs and folding my arms, thinking for a split second whether to tell him about last night. A second longer of thought made me change my mind. We weren't tight. We didn't share intimate details of our lives and that wasn't going to change now.

"At the moment, no. I'm done with what I had to do before, so I came to see if there was something else you needed help with."

He sighed and leaned back, his elbows resting on the arms of his chair, and his fingers clasped together. There was a slight frown on his face, and I took it to mean I wasn't going to particularly like the news he had to tell me.

"There's a deal we need to get for the hotel, an important deal. The problem is, I'm swamped with meetings for today, besides everything else I need to do."

"And?" I asked out of curiosity.

He picked up a folder on top of his desk and pushed it across to me.

"We either get it, or our competitors will pick it up from under us, and we can't have that or Dad will have palpitations when he comes back. I need you to go and get this deal for us."

I read through the document, taking note of the dates. Trent was right; Dad would be mad if we lost this because it was a deal he must have been working on for nearly three months. I recognized some of the names, and they were pretty big, almost as big as the Thompson name.

"How long do you think it'll take you?" Trent prompted, his eyes drilling into me.

"It'll only take a day or two. It depends on the level of competition though, because with something like this I'm assuming there *is* going to be competition."

He knew more about it than I did. I had to pick his brains, even if my cock was begging me to find Laura. My mind was telling me I couldn't fuck this up. Not once, if for once I was going to earn my Dad's respect. Even if it felt like a waste of time at the best of times.

"There is, but I'm sure it's not anything you can't deal with. I need you to head out as soon as possible. I would have gone myself, but I get better deals out of a board-room, and Kevin isn't particularly suited to this."

Of the three of us, I was the one good at cutting deals. I closed the folder and got up.

"I'll head out in an hour. I'll let you know when I get the deal."

"Or you could let me know if it falls through."

I laughed. "Oh, please. I've never lost on a deal."

Especially not when it was taking up my time when

there was plenty of other shit I could have been doing. I left the office with the folder tucked under my arm, heading back to my room. Once I was in, I picked up the hotel phone and made a call to the cleaning department.

I had a small suitcase packed by the time the door to my room was unlocked, and Laura came in, pulling in her cleaning supplies. She looked up, her eyes widening in shock to see I was still in there, but then they narrowed on me.

"Sorry for calling you in," I said with a sheepish smile. "I didn't know how else to meet you. When did you leave my room this morning?"

She arched an eyebrow. "I got up pretty early to head home to get showered and changed first. Was that all you wanted to ask?"

I wanted to cross the space between us and pull her into my arms for a long, wet kiss. The tenseness in her shoulders and almost defensive stance stopped me. I didn't know why she was on edge and I didn't like that. I wanted to frown but didn't want her to think something was wrong, so I pasted on a smile and tucked my hands into my pockets, clenching them into fists.

"There was something else." I sighed. "My brother is sending me on a little errand out of town. He's too busy here and it's not something Kevin can do, so it's up to me."

I was trying to sound important because part of me felt like an errand boy and the other part was trying to convince myself that it would come to an end once I closed this deal.

She looked around the room. "You didn't have to call

me up here just for that. There isn't even that much of a mess here, and I do have a job to do."

"I know, but I don't have your number, and I wanted to let you know that I'll be back, I'm not gone for good yet."

"Not yet, huh," she teased, a slight grin on her face.

"Yeah, not yet," I said with a chuckle. "Besides that, I wanted you to know… that I would like to see you again."

I must have surprised her with that declaration because she had this stunned look on her face like she hadn't expected me to want more from her than one night. That was far from the case; I wanted much more than a single night with this woman.

"I need to head out now," I said, turning back to the bedroom to retrieve my suitcase. "I'll see you when I get back!"

I pecked a kiss on her cheek, then left the room like a lovesick teenager. Once I got downstairs there was a car waiting for me. I hopped in and the driver took me to a small airstrip. Trent had arranged for everything, perfect as usual.

On the ride there, I sat back in my seat and looked over the documents some more. I hated being unprepared and the ride would give me that time if I used it properly, then I would have the confidence to do what I needed to do on landing. Besides, I knew better than to use my phone on the plane. When I'd gone through the whole document thoroughly, I tilted my head back and closed my eyes for a bit of rest.

When the plane landed, I got off and was led to a

waiting car that drove me to the hotel I'd be staying in for the night. I went straight to my room, getting out my phone for a quick round of searches. An hour later, I was as ready as I was going to be on such short notice and left the room.

Before I could talk to my targets, I had to find them. I'd learned just enough about their hobbies and habits to know where to find them. In the lobby, I picked some pamphlets up of the hotel and went through them quickly.

"First off," I muttered, "the lounge."

Trent would have let them know I was on the way. The meeting would be super casual, which pretty much meant we could end up anywhere. It was time for lunch, so they'd be about ready to eat, I thought. Lucky for me, I didn't have to wait long to meet them, because they were in the hotel lounge like I'd thought they would be, all gathered together and talking loudly in a circle of seats.

"Good afternoon, gentlemen," I said smoothly, cutting into the conversation. "Would you mind very much if I joined you?"

"Why, if it isn't Matthew's second son?" one of the men said, his hand out for mine. I took it and looked him over.

I recognized him, and a few of the others, because they'd worked with my dad before. I was probably the youngest guy in the whole group, but that didn't stop them from letting me off easy, simply because of my last name and my dad. There were some guys I recognized as the competition as well, and I wondered how much of a head start they had on me.

Not that it was going to matter. If Dad wanted this deal, I was going to get it for him.

"Hey," one of the guys said, "it's lunch already, so why don't we all go eat now?"

There was a round of agreement, and everyone got up to go to the hotel's restaurant. We were a pretty large group, but it was full of big names, so we were served well enough.

I was barely paying that much attention to the proceedings, though I'd done this often enough there was nothing I missed in the discussions, and I even joined in at times. It was all so fucking casual it would take a while before any actual talking about the deal went down. I couldn't be the first to bring it up either, or I was going to lose.

Throughout the whole thing, I found myself preoccupied. After lounging around a bit after lunch to let the food settle, the group moved to the tennis courts for a few rounds. I didn't have anything casual to change into, but besides rugby, there wasn't any sport I played so I wouldn't be joining in any way. Instead, I sat to the side with the commentators, dropping a few lines here and there.

Afterward, we all went to a club not too far from the hotel. The second I walked into the room, I knew just what kind of club it was. Usually, I would have been right in my element, but I couldn't help but look at the others as we settled into the VIP area, half-naked women all over the room perking up at the group, offering themselves freely.

Fuck!

Usually, that would be the first thing on my mind. I would walk up to the bevy of beautiful women, or they'd come swarming to me like bees, but I had the honey back home and she wasn't here. There was only one woman I wanted right now, and I sat back like a chump with a limp dick knowing that no matter what, none of the women here could get *it* or even me in the mood right now.

12

MASON

"Hey, Thompson! Would you get us some drinks?"

I started at the call, though I came back to myself in the next second, a smile crossing my face.

"Everybody tell me what you want," I said, getting up. "I'll have it all brought over."

I wasn't surprised they were asking me to go, I was surprised they hadn't tried to send me on errands sooner, considering how much younger I was than anyone else in the group. They were all above twenty-five, and I was only twenty-three. I was going to be treated as the gopher, but not for long if I could help it.

Even in the VIP area, the place was crowded, and it was enough to let me know the club was fairly popular in the area. There was a bar set up against one wall, and I slid through the bodies moving around easily. Women came at me because I was young, tall and handsome. Being in the VIP area also gave me importance, so that meant I was worth something, namely their time to try and get my money out of my pockets and into theirs. It was pretty much the same thing that happened to me any time I walked into a club, only this time, I didn't bother stopping to look at any of them.

None of them were my type, then again neither was Laura. I was surprised that now I'd had a taste of her, I couldn't get her out of my mind. She was incredible.

It was a little maddening. The whole time since I'd left the hotel, I hadn't been able to get her out of my mind. I would have loved to bring her on the trip with me, to have her on my arm the whole time. Not that I would have even if she'd agreed to come with me. It may or may not have helped the deal I needed to make, and I had to think carefully about everything. If I didn't have the experience I did, the attention I was paying to this whole deal would not have been enough.

"Hey," I called out to the bartender. "I'd like a few drinks brought to our table? Over there." I gestured back to where I'd come from over my shoulder.

"Sure. What is it you'd like?"

The bartender folded her arms on top of the bar, leaning over it to bring her face closer to mine and flash some cleavage. My eyes drifted down for a second, before looking up into her heated eyes and flirtatious smile. Any other time, I would have flirted back. Even in the middle of a deal, I wouldn't have held myself back.

All I could think about when I looked at this woman, was how her dark hair was completely different from Laura's fair locks. Her eyes were darker, her skin paler, her body thinner. She was completely different from Laura, and while it wasn't off-putting, it didn't get my body hot either.

"Just the drinks!" I said listing off the orders.

She took the hint and backed off. "I'll have it all sent to your table, sir. Please wait a few minutes."

I nodded, then turned to head back.

Laura…

Last night with her had been full of surprises in several ways. While Laura giving into me was one of them, there was more than that. Now that I was away from her, I couldn't help wondering…

All she'd told me was that she had been sick, but it wouldn't need a genius to know that she'd likely had breast cancer at some point. I knew all about it because it was one of the causes my mom donated to over the years, and the couple times I'd helped her out in her fundraisers, I'd learned bits and pieces.

Just hearing the word cancer was bad enough. Laura was lucky to be alive. I knew some of the statistics, and how they weren't all that reassuring for someone in that position. It was difficult to connect the perky, sassy maid with such an illness. She didn't act like someone who'd been through something like that, because I knew it couldn't have been simple, considering the extent of the surgery and the lingering scars I'd seen on her body.

I made it back to where the group was, and not long after the drinks followed. Not long after that the women came, but every time I looked at one of them, all I could see was Laura in my mind. In particular, the look on her face when I made her explode, feeling her body shaking under mine as she shuddered in orgasm. Fuck, I could still taste her on my tongue.

Some time passed, and I noticed some of the men in our group getting up to join the women on the dance floor. A few of them stayed behind to enjoy the drinks, and I decided to pay some extra attention.

"You've been quiet, Mason," one of the men said and I hated that someone else had observed my behavior. I just wanted to be left alone. A drink or two and then I was out of here. I wasn't going to win the deal in this place.

"I'm not particularly in a partying mood, I suppose," I said, surprised at my own honesty.

"Ah, yes. I heard the rumors that your father isn't well? Who's managing the business in his place?"

"My brothers and I are looking after things, but Trent is at the forefront of it all."

Fuck! I hated to use my Dad's illness as an excuse, but it was better than telling him what was really on my mind.

"Ah, yes. The oldest Thompson son. So he's back to work for your father?"

"He's always worked for the family, really. We all have. Dad just likes to get most things done on his own. My brother would have come but he told me he'd be in meetings for the whole day, so I came in his place."

He nodded his head and shared looks with his associate.

"I'm going to assume you came here to make a deal then?"

This was it. While the VIP section of a club wasn't

exactly a convenient place to make deals, it didn't matter. The others were off having fun, and I stayed back to make my case for the deal. The others might have had chances throughout the day, before I joined the group when they were playing tennis, even on the drive to the club. I wouldn't know who got the deal until tomorrow, but I was fairly confident in my abilities.

It was the one thing Dad had to be proud of when it came to me.

Laura was still in my thoughts, but I pushed them aside. As much as I wanted to go back to her, I needed to focus on closing the deal.

By the time the others came back to join us, I was done negotiating. I didn't last long after that, before I was impatient to be away from all the noise and smell of alcohol.

"If you'll all excuse me," I said, getting up. "I'm going to be heading back."

No one tried to get me to stay. In fact, some of the competition grinned when they heard I was leaving. Not that I cared. I made my way back to the hotel where I took a shower then lay down on the bed. It was a while before I could fall asleep.

The next morning, I got the good news just before I checked out of the hotel. We got the deal. I was grinning all the way back home because I finished my task, and I would get to see Laura. I was in a hurry to relay the news to Trent, then I could find Laura and get back to my own life. When I arrived at the hotel, I had my suitcase taken to my room for me and took the elevator all the way up to the office. Trent was always in there. He even ate lunch in the office, so it never occurred to me that I wouldn't find him there.

"What?"

I looked up at the secretary; my hand paused on the door handle. She stood up from her desk and rounded it to stand in front of me. I backed up for a moment.

"Is my brother busy somewhere else? A meeting?" I didn't quite believe her when she said he was out.

She shook her head, her hands clasped together in front of her stomach and a small furrow in her brow.

"Mr. Thompson left, I'm afraid."

An eyebrow jumped up. "My brother left? The hotel? Is it for work, or what?"

I was getting impatient and hating all this fucking cloak and dagger treatment. Just tell me what's going on and be done. Why is everyone always so fucking secretive?

"Your sister came to meet him, and they spoke. After- ward, he checked out of the hotel."

I frowned, glanced at the door, then turned back down the hallway, pulling my phone out of my pocket to call my sister. It took so long for her to pick up I almost thought she'd ignore me. She picked up just before the call cut off.

"What is it?" she asked, her voice subdued.

It was enough to give me a moment's pause. I wanted to ask what was wrong, but I had something much more important to deal with.

"Emily, I heard Trent took off after you said something to him. What the hell happened while I was away? And where's Kevin?"

She sighed. "I think Kevin is still busy, but Trent's gone

back home. To his home, not the mansion. If you want to know why, you'll want to ask him, but he dropped everything and left."

That had me freezing again. Fuck, there was still work to be done, wasn't there? Especially with this new deal coming in. I couldn't call Trent and ask why he'd just left, he and I weren't nearly that close. But he'd pretty much left Kevin and me in charge without a word. It wasn't like him and it meant I'd be busier now, instead of taking some time off. I let out a groan, looking at the folder I still held in my hand where I'd the signed documents for the deal.

"I've gotta go, Emily. I need to get some stuff done here. I'll call you later so we can talk."

I would have liked to ignore all responsibility and play hooky, but I knew better. The hotel would survive without someone working in the head office for a day but work still needed to get done. Damn our father and his stupid work ethic. I turned around and walked back to the secretary.

"Is there anything important Trent was supposed to do before he left? I'll do it myself."

"Yes, sir," she said, getting back up. "Please come this way, and I'll show you."

I sighed as I followed her into the office, knowing my schedule would be packed for the rest of the day. I could call Kevin later to let him know so we could divide the work up equally.

. . .

IT WAS evening by the time I sat back in the office chair, done with… not everything but enough that I thought I could get some rest and continue with everything else later. Laura immediately came to mind, and I jumped out of my seat.

I'd spent most of yesterday and today just thinking about her, wanting to see her. I'd turned down all the women who'd come onto me on my trip, very tempting women at that. Not one of them had been able to make me stop thinking of Laura just by looking at them. They also didn't have that spark that attracted me to Laura so much in the first place. That something that made my toes curl every time she was in my vicinity.

After I'd had her in my bed, my interest in her had increased rather than waned. Instead of summoning her to my room again, because she very clearly didn't like it, I went out to look for her.

13

LAURA

I finished my last room of the day and sighed as I rolled my trolley of supplies back to the elevator. I was so darn tired today. It was probably because I knew Mason was around, even though I hadn't seen him yet. Since he'd called me to his room a few times, my work schedule had been moved around so I was working on his floor permanently now.

No way was I going to tell him that. As if he wasn't the reason I'd been reassigned in the first place. I knew the day he got back from his trip, and I couldn't help feeling anxious about it. That was three days ago and still, I couldn't help the anxiety every time I went into work and I blamed it all on that boy.

I hadn't seen him. Not once. I figured he was busy. It hadn't taken long after it happened for the rumor about Trent leaving the hotel to spread around. No one knew why though. I imagined Mason was filling in his brother's work.

I should have been relieved not to have to face him yet, so why did I feel so disappointed? After I went to his room to do my job, only to see his suitcase already in there, the same one I'd seen him leave with, I'd been super jumpy about running into him in the hall as I worked. I really should consider myself lucky that he wasn't searching me out, because I needed to nip what I'd started with him in the bud before I fell in too deep.

I couldn't help the way I was feeling right now, it was kind of crazy. A few days ago, I didn't want any man near me. I was happy living and just enjoying life. The one I thought I wouldn't have ever again after the cancer struck. I never in my wildest dreams imagined being with some-one. Especially someone as hot as Mason.

I sighed again as the elevator doors opened to the first floor, and wheeled my supplies to the storeroom where all the cleaning stuff was kept. I left it all there, then went to the lockers to get changed quickly. It was past time I clocked out already, and even with the disappointment, I wasn't going to stick around in case Mason came looking for me.

I headed out of the hotel, quickly, like I was running from something. My walk home was a bit more subdued than usual. I kept picking up speed when I remembered to, or when I crossed the road, but for most of the way, I was preoccupied. I'd been preoccupied ever since I woke up to find myself in Mason's arms after our night together. I kept thinking about how I hadn't wanted to move from the bed, but I'd done it anyway because I had to.

The fiasco between Trent and Jessi came into my mind,

and it was enough to get me running. Something I rarely did—I wasn't the type that loved to exercise, even though they said it was crucial to my recovery to get exercise, slowly at first and then increase it. It was on my to-do list but lately, the only thing that was on my mind was Mason and now Jessi. What happened to Jessi?

How could I possibly forget my friend? For the one night, sure, it was part of what pushed me to accept Mason's hand when he held it out to me in the first place. It hadn't been the whole reason, but still.

Jessi was gone.

Even worse, if the rumors of her setting up a transfer with the manager hadn't become a rumor, she might have left without letting me know beforehand. She didn't even say goodbye, I just got into work that day, and when I looked for her I couldn't find her.

She hadn't explicitly stated it, but I knew the reason she felt she had to leave was because of Trent. She hadn't told me exactly what happened between the two of them that changed things, but that was my mistake. If I'd asked her and prompted her to tell me at least we would have talked before she left. Heck, I might have talked her out of transferring to a different hotel branch. I knew where she'd gone, and it wasn't like I couldn't visit her. That would have to wait because any trips would have to be when I had the time to spare, and the trip would have to be more than one day because it was so far away. She wasn't close by anymore.

Even worse was knowing that her move was prompted by Trent, Mason's brother. I couldn't say I knew the guy;

we'd only met that one time after all. Not that I was sure he even noticed because his eyes had been all for Jessi. Yet, now that Jessi was gone, even without knowing the reason, I resented him a little. As unfair as it was, I resented Mason by extension for sharing the guy's blood. Only a little bit though.

More than anything, watching how things went down between them made me realize I didn't want the same for myself. So while I might have had a moment of weakness when Mason showed up at my most vulnerable moment and started acting nice to me, I couldn't allow it to happen a second time.

Mason was hot, young, and rich. Women threw themselves at him because they were attracted to one or a combination of the three. I knew eventually he'd want someone younger and closer to his status, not a lowly maid.

Someone that could have children, something I didn't think would be for me. Not that I lacked confidence in my body to carry to term, as long as the cancer didn't come back, I was entirely healthy. I just lacked enough faith in Mason to have that kind of relationship.

With Jessi gone, there wasn't anyone else that I was nearly so close with at the hotel, or in the area that I could talk to about this sort of thing. I missed my friend, so the moment I made it home and into my apartment, I was whipping my phone out and settling comfortably into the couch, hopefully for a long conversation.

She answered on the second ring.

"Laura, hey!"

My eyebrow jumped up at her tone of voice. It was strangely perky, especially considering she'd almost sounded miserable the last few times I called her.

"Jessi?" I said tentatively. "Is everything all right?"

"Oh, everything is perfect! But tell me, did you want to talk about something? Your voice sounds a little strange."

I was surprised but only for a moment, then I broke into a little giggle.

"You know me better than anyone else, don't you?" I quipped, already feeling better just hearing my friend's voice so upbeat.

"And you know me best, too," she chirped. "I'm pretty sure you know me even better than my parents. They pretty much had to focus more on work than me growing up, so I'm really glad we're friends."

My eyes narrowed in suspicion. "Okay, something is up. Why are you suddenly waxing poetic about our friendship?"

"It's not waxing poetic! I'm just telling the truth."

"Yeah, but it's also not quite like you, and I'm feeling a little worried here. Seriously, did something happen?"

"Shouldn't I be asking you that?" she pointed out. "Your voice sounds heavy, like you have something important to tell me. Did something happen at the hotel? You can talk to me, you know? You're always telling me that, let me do it for a change."

I wanted to tell her all about Mason's sudden interest in me, how I'd found myself cleaning up his room daily while trying to avoid him at the same time, about the two of us sleeping together. Instead, a sigh escaped my lips, and I leaned back in the chair. She sounded pretty excited, and it had been a while since I heard her sound so happy. I didn't want to ruin it over something so minor when I could always tell her some other time.

"Nothing much," I said with a sigh. "Things around here are just a little dull without you."

"You could always use the opportunity to make more close friends?" she said, sounding exasperated. "Hell, there's always Emily to keep you company!"

"I think she's a little busy these days, and I just don't click with any of the other staff like I do with you," I said honestly. "I just wish you were still here. I've missed you."

There was a short pause, then the sound of giggles and my eyebrows shot up. Something definitely must have made her happy for her to sound like that.

"Hey," she said, tone slightly teasing. "Guess what?"

"What?" I asked, a little suspicious and impatient because I hated guessing games. "Something good happened, but what was it?"

"You won't have to miss me anymore!" she said, laughing.

My mind blanked, and it took me a minute to understand what she meant. Then my eyes widened, and I let out a gasp.

"Don't tell me…!"

"I'm on my way back!" she squealed. "Trent came to the beach hotel to ask me to come back, and I said yes."

My eyes went impossibly wider. "He did what?!"

"I have no idea why he even did it, it was such a surprise to me too, you know? Anyway, don't worry, I will be back home soon, so you won't have time to miss me for much longer, all right?"

"Jessi, that's wonderful! Surprising and completely unexpected, but I know it's what you want, right? You're giving this guy a chance?"

She went quiet for a moment, and when she spoke again she sounded pensive.

"It's weird, isn't it? Even after all those times I told myself there was no damn way anything could happen between him and me. I just called it a miracle and decided to roll with it. It feels kind of like getting an old friend back. Did I tell you that Trent and I grew up with each other?"

"Hmm," I hummed, thinking back. "Come to think of it, did you? You didn't give me many details about the two of you."

"Oh, yeah. I didn't feel like talking about him before, but if there's something you want to hear, I'm all for it right now."

"There's one thing I've been curious about," I said, once she gave her confirmation. "Tell me all that happened between you and Trent from the day you found out he was coming back, to the two of you meeting for the first time in years."

I shifted so I lay back on the arm of the couch with pillows cushioned under me, settling in comfortably for what I felt would be a long talk with my best friend.

14

LAURA

Jessi was back! In spite of everything, even with how anxious and depressed I'd become since she'd left, now she was back I was my usual self once more. Happy and bubbly, carrying both emotions wherever I went.

Not that I wasn't still anxious when it came to Mason, though. I'd decided it would be in everyone's best interest if I cut ties with Mason before things became too sticky. Jessi was on the road to her happy ending with Trent, and I was happy for her. Just because it worked for her with the eldest Thompson brother, didn't mean I could wish for the same from Mason, however.

I'd pretty much used up all my miracles just being healthy. Getting too entangled with Mason could not lead to anything good.

For one, he was nothing like his brother. Trent acted a lot like his father, something of a workaholic like he didn't know how to relax. I knew now he was with Jessi, he'd be taking time off now and then. She'd make sure of it, even though he was technically our boss, because she was a caring woman like that.

Mason, on the other hand… all the staff in the hotel, be they maids, or staff in the kitchen, the lobby, on the grounds… everyone knew just what kind of person Mason was, and it wasn't the kind of person that you could rely on in a serious relationship.

He liked to party. A lot. I'd known that already. Heck, I was always there to clean up his messes for him, and several times I got to see just how out of hand those parties could get. In every single one, there was never a time I'd found him fully clothed or without some woman hanging off him. After I slept with him, those images came back to haunt me, and I couldn't help but regret what I'd done a little bit.

It had been my decision, but after a long time of deliberating, I realized it had been the wrong one. Mason's life was one I didn't think I could live up to, and not just because we were in different social classes and he had way more now than I ever would working on my own for the rest of my life.

Avoiding him was hard on me. I handled it for a week without actually running into him, and I didn't know if it was down to luck, or if he was just really busy.

I made sure to clean his room later, but not too late. And while I worked on his floor, I tried to spend as little time in the hallway as possible, working faster than I ever had before. It was detrimental in that I got to spend more time in the staff lounge and risked him finding me there again, or I landed myself more work for having extra time for other duties before I clocked out. At least Jessi was back and she was always there to keep me company.

In all that time, I hadn't caught even a single glimpse of Mason, but it didn't make me happy at all. I was losing my usual cheer and everyone was starting to notice. So to keep them off my tail, I'd pretend. Fake cheeriness was something I hated because I'd done it so much when I was sick and didn't want my college friends to know what was going on with me. I went home each night and I wanted to cry myself to sleep. I didn't know why because I shouldn't already feel attached to this guy. Before the night we spent together, I'd only caught glimpses of him, sometimes in the nude. It wasn't like we were close.

It was for the best. Still, when I trudged into work at the one-week mark of avoidance, it was with heavy feet and an even heavier heart. I was early because I'd woken up early, and when I walked into the staff room, I heard someone humming, and immediately knew it was Jessi.

"Someone's in a good mood today," I called out to the kitchen, heading that way. It was early, so I didn't need to change into my uniform just yet.

"Someone's in a not so good mood today," she retorted, smiling at me over her shoulder.

"Are you baking right now?"

"Yeah. I had the time and you've been so down lately. I wanted to make you something sweet. Also, it's an experiment. I'm trying out some new creations. Matthew Thompson asked for it himself, so I've been working myself to the bone coming up with it."

That had me perking right up. Usually when Jessi came up with new creations, it could take a while before she was happy with what she wanted to make, and in the meantime, there were plenty of treats to enjoy. Usually, I didn't indulge myself in too much sugar or desserts, but I never refused one of Jessi's.

"Can I try some now? Are you making enough for everyone, or...?"

"Yeah. My kitchen isn't big enough for this, and I usually either work at my parent's place or here, but it would have to be past hours and I'd be using the hotel's ingredients. Trent had everything I needed be stocked up. I'll be sending some of this up to his office later, and he'll probably share them with his family. He'll have to agree before anything can be added to the menu."

I sniffed the air a little, already drooling at the scent. There was a hint of mango in there, some vanilla, and I wondered at exactly what she was trying to make. She picked out one of the pastries from the tray with a napkin and held it out to me. It was shaped like a pie, but small enough to fit in my hand with a dip at the top, where icing had been sprinkled.

"Careful. I took that batch out of the oven just a few minutes ago, so it's probably still hot."

"It feels fine to me through the napkin, not hot or anything."

Still, I brought it cautiously to my mouth. Never once had I tasted something Jessi made and not liked it. I'd tried experimenting with cooking on my own sometimes, and it always came out badly, so even if she was my friend, I always approached experiments with caution.

Jessi was good at her job. I bit into the pastry, and my eyes widened at the burst of flavor on my tongue. There was a fusion of mango and vanilla, and maybe something else in there, then the soft pastry and the sweet icing.

"This tastes amazing," I said, chowing down on the rest of it, then holding my hand out for more.

She laughed. "Well, I would hope so, considering our boss will taste it. I've been trying to get a solid recipe for this for the past few days. The first ones…"

"Weren't as great?" I guessed.

Another reason why the stuff she made tasted so good; she usually went through all the trials on her own before having someone else try out the semi-finished product. She turned herself into her own guinea pig.

"They weren't terrible but I burnt some of them. Then I ended up eating them anyway because I just hate to waste food and effort."

She picked another one for me, then one for herself, and took a tiny bite, chewing with a small frown on her face.

"It's not bad… but it's still missing something. It doesn't have to be perfect, but I need it to be good enough for the hotel's standards in case we get another surprise review."

"Your food always gets nice reviews anyway. You don't have anything to worry about."

"There's always something to worry about. Everybody's a critic these days, and I don't like hearing people didn't like my stuff."

"If this is going to have a lot of sugar, though…"

"I'll figure something out for a sugar-free category. There's only so healthy you can make any dessert, and that one will probably take me longer to work out. Also, I need to take in possible allergies, so I'm watching the ingredients I put in…"

I watched her in admiration. "You take your job seriously."

She laughed. "Of course I do! I spent a lot of time and money to get to where I am. I wouldn't waste so much effort if it were something I hated. Besides, it's great when I get to taste my food." Then she laughed again, a little more rueful as she glanced down at herself. "I do have to worry about my weight with all the pastries and desserts I keep eating."

"Exercise more. It's why I usually walk, though if you wanted, you could try going to the gym."

At the word 'gym,' Jessi almost looked pained, and I laughed at her reaction. As much as she worried about her weight with what she loved to eat, she disliked the gym. I'd be making time to go myself but I ate pretty healthily, and while I was curvy, I wasn't quite as plump as Jessi was. She was self-conscious about it but I thought it looked good on her.

"So," she said after we'd eaten a couple more. "What's been going on with you lately? You're not acting like your usual self at all."

Now that she'd brought it up, I couldn't help feeling down again, my shoulders slumping as I let out a weary sigh.

"I've just… been having problems."

She smiled. "I realize that. And because you did the same for me, I won't push you for details until you want to tell me on your own."

I gave her a grateful smile back, though it was touched with unease. I didn't know why I hadn't told her yet. It had bugged me before when I knew something had happened between her and Trent, and she didn't tell me about it, but every time I'd opened my mouth to try and broach the subject, I'd say something else instead.

"It's not something to worry about," I reassured her. "It's just something I need to get over."

Mason would not become my whole life. I had a lot that was great in my life without him. Even if he was hot as hell, and just the thought of him made me want to stay in bed some mornings, I could and would move on.

15

MASON

They say that time flies when you're having fun and drags when you're not. It fucking did because I felt as if I hadn't seen Laura in years and it had only been a fucking week. I'd really fallen hard for her. I thought that this sort of shit only happens in those chick flicks Emily watches.

Even with Trent back and helping out again, there was still too much to do. I hated to admit that I'd valued myself as being a workaholic and I'd been far from it lately. I couldn't help it if unlike him, I didn't spend all my time in the office sitting down in front of papers and a computer all day. In the short time I'd covered for him, there'd been plenty of stuff I'd overlooked, so technically, my being so busy was just because I was cleaning up my mess. Still, I didn't like it.

I also didn't like that it felt like Laura was avoiding me. Even when I'd called to have her come to my room, I was informed she was now cleaning my room, permanently. She probably just did it at a time when she knew I wouldn't be in the room, and though I'd tried to surprise her a few times, I never caught her.

Fuck, I missed Laura as if a part of me was missing, like a drug addict needing a fix. I hated being fucking needy, but I was becoming just that.

"This isn't going to end," I muttered to myself as I got out of bed and headed for the bathroom, in a terrible mood for the fourth day in a row. Then I sighed. "It's kinda my fault I still don't have her phone number."

After taking a shower, I got dressed. Since it was still pretty early, I sat in my living room and had some orange juice from the fridge. I didn't feel like breakfast. I was also waking up way earlier than I was used to and having trouble falling asleep.

How could one woman have left my world so upside down, and only after one night together? I didn't get hung up on women, especially ones that didn't want me again after they had me. From what I remembered, she'd enjoyed our time together, even if she'd been a little subdued afterward. I guessed she was tired, but maybe... Did she regret it?

No!

I didn't know why Laura was avoiding me—and she was, because of the two of us, she was the one who knew how to contact me. I wasn't going to let things stand as they were. I was used to getting whatever I wanted; and while that was a pretty fucking spoiled thought, it was true, and I wasn't about to break it just yet. Not now when the one thing I wanted was Laura. She wasn't an object to be owned, and I knew better than anyone that money didn't buy affections. She didn't seem like she'd be swayed like most of the women I met, but I had to try something.

I'd warned Emily all our lives about making friends with the help, but I no longer cared. If she came to me to snark about it, I would take it quietly and leave her relationships alone. I wanted Laura, and even if we were from different worlds, I was going to try.

I didn't fucking care about the age gap, but I had a feeling that she did. It wasn't like she was seventy or something! She was only thirty-five. Sure, that was still more than a decade older than me, but she hardly looked her age, it had been a surprise for me to hear it.

"I need some help," I decided, jumping up from the couch.

I was done moping around and waiting for her to find me. I was going to take some action. Then I paused, wondering exactly what I could do to get a woman to fall for me. Usually, they came to me of their own free will, but I'd never had to actually woo a woman. Even back in high school and all through college.

For a moment, I thought of calling my sister for advice. That was a bad idea, and I vetoed it almost immediately. There was Mom, but she was almost just as bad. If either of them found out there was a woman I was trying to win over, not only would they tease me over it, they'd demand and pry to know who it was until I caved. I wasn't worried about their reactions exactly; I just didn't want my family butting into my love life.

Since the family was out of the question, I pulled out my phone and did some searches online to find what I needed. I saw several sites and found a few things on repeat. They were simple enough to accomplish. I switched my searches to local areas, looking for flower shops, candy, and fashion stores.

Over the next few days, I had things sent to her. I didn't know her home address, and I didn't want to abuse the fact that I was the boss's son and could easily get her information. So all the gifts passed through the staff lounge. I couldn't spare much time to go there myself at the times I assumed she'd be there, but I could do this much.

Trent kept working me to the bone, and I kept sending present after present in my new campaign to win this woman over. I never attached my name and tried to make the deliveries as discreet as possible so people wouldn't talk. She'd be more affected by the rumors than I would be, after all. Flowers, candy, other expensive gifts; everything I thought a woman would want.

I was mistaken though, because in my moment of frustration and desperation, I forgot how Laura was unlike any of the women I'd ever hooked up with before. She didn't appreciate any of the gifts, and over the week I'd sent them, they were returned. Every single one. I wasn't sure what it was she disliked, so I tried changing things up, but still, nothing. She also didn't send word as to why she refused everything.

It all left me so fucking frustrated. It was all I could do not to scream my head off.

"What was that?"

"Huh?" I blinked as I looked up and for once thought about something else apart from Laura.

Ah. I was sitting in the office, where Trent had the desk I'd used before brought back in for me. Moving around would probably have been better for my frustration, but I was probably beyond even that already. Only seeing Laura or getting some answers to the mounting questions—most of them varying ways of asking just what it was that she wanted—would get me to calm down.

"Is something wrong?" Trent said. "You've been muttering to yourself over there, and I don't know if you're cursing me for giving you too much work, or what. Work that I'm pretty sure you aren't even doing."

I blinked at the desk in front of me, feeling a little confused. He was right. For a moment, I almost felt ashamed. Then I remembered I was Mason Thompson. While this scene was eerily a lot like my times in high school, sitting at my desk with work I was ignoring in favor of looking over my phone underneath it, even back then I'd never felt anything but annoyance at being interrupted.

"Sorry about that. You're right. I'm just a little distracted."

I let out a sigh, dropping my phone on the desk as I leaned back in my chair, running an agitated hand through my hair.

"Do you want to talk about it?"

My head snapped up, eyes wide as I looked over at my brother. "What?"

Trent folded his arms on the desk, leaning forward slightly with an open expression.

"Seriously, tell me what it is. It might make you feel better to talk about it."

I snorted. "I doubt it." Then I narrowed my eyes at him. "And you and I don't have the relationship where we share things, Trent. Not personal things, anyway."

He shrugged, nodding as he conceded the point. "That's true, and it's probably entirely my fault. But I'm still your big brother and I've got years of experience on you. I might be of some help."

I wanted to tell him that the fault wasn't entirely his own. A great part of it was Dad's fault.

"It's just… something's been frustrating me lately. It's something I'll work through eventually on my own. I just… have to keep trying, right?"

"Does it have anything to do with Dad?"

"Huh?" I repeated with a blank expression.

Trent had this pensive look on his face that I couldn't read. I wondered what he was thinking.

"I was wondering whether or not I should tell you guys. Or even if I should tell you. As far as I know, Kevin is still in the dark. Not that I was trying to hide it from you, I just… didn't know how to bring it up."

I frowned, momentarily distracted. "What are you talking about? What don't Kevin and I know?"

Trent sighed, then leaned back in his chair and folded his arms across his chest. "Well, it's this thing about Dad.

Remember how we were all told he had a heart attack and he wasn't well?" He paused, so I nodded, prompting him to go on. "As it turns out, that's not exactly true. Dad is just fine. I heard it, and I didn't want to believe it, but this is Dad. So I left, and he came to talk me into coming back after that. He told me to keep working because he was enjoying his vacation."

His expression once he finished was calm. I blinked at him for a moment, not sure whether or not I should just take his word for it. Trent was waiting for a reaction from me. At first, I didn't know how I should react, but slowly, it was sinking in for me, and I was not happy with the trick Dad had pulled on us.

I almost lost it right then and there, despite Trent's calm attitude. There was a lot of shit on the desk in front of me; some documents I was meant to look through, a computer had been given to me to use. All of it so I could work for my father, who I'd momentarily forgotten as thoughts of Laura took over my mind. It hadn't even occurred to me just how long it had been since I last asked to see him only to be rebuffed.

If I was honest, I wasn't even surprised. I'd already suspected as much. For a man at death's door to suddenly refuse to see his children was odd, and I'm many things but stupid isn't one of them. I don't know why I hadn't demanded an answer before now, yet here I was, totally not shocked to be told I'd been made a fool of by my father. Again.

Right then, I was well past super frustrated and somehow, I simply wasn't in the mood to be smug that I'd almost guessed right. I was pissed off, righteously so, and in a move that I suspected mirrored what Trent did when he found out, I left everything where it was and walked out of the office.

Trent didn't call me back, not that I would have stopped if he did. He probably knew, so he didn't bother.

16

MASON

"For crying out loud, Dad!"

I stomped down the hallway because I was fed up. Everything was one big mess and it didn't seem to be getting any better. I didn't need this stress in my life.

How could the old man do this to me? To all of us! Whatever his reasons for lying, I was worried about him when I'd decided to go back home. It wasn't like he never saw me around! Unlike Trent, the prodigal son, and Kevin, the wanderer, I went home a little too much considering I didn't have to. Maybe that was the issue. I was a sucker for punishment. Then again it was more for the sake of Mom and Emily, but it wasn't like I didn't have time for Dad on those trips. I was at the mansion six month ago, and I'd stuck around for a whole two weeks.

What more did he want?

I'd acted like a fucking child, doing everything he'd asked, and for what?

Fuck all!

I quit rugby to learn the ropes of the business. I didn't like it, but I went along anyway because he wanted me to. He had me going all over the place to take care of hotel dealings. He didn't do that with Kevin. Or Trent for that matter.

When I'd heard that he wasn't well, I didn't think foul play, but then again why should that have been the first thing that came into my mind? I pretty much put my life on hold just to come back for Dad. I was living at the hotel because I thought it would be better than sticking around the mansion. I hate commutes. I had my own home, though in another town where I would have rather lived quietly, as ridiculous as that sounded for me with all the parties I kept having and attending.

Still, it wasn't like I'd had intentions of living that way my whole life. No matter how angry I was with my dad. Besides, a part of me didn't like the constant parties. All I did was get wasted and lose even more precious time.

I fucking hated it, I suddenly realized. I hated all of it, staying at the mansion, even my suite room at the hotel was a waste. I'd grown up with money, sure, but the one thing they never tell you about mansions and huge hotel rooms is that the space is too big, too cold. A little too much like the boarding school for me to be comfortable, but then I'd scraped through that in the end.

I made it to the elevator without meeting anyone's gaze, then pressed the button to take me down to my floor. Once the elevator stopped, I walked quickly to my room and let myself in, then headed straight for the bedroom.

"Ugh," I groaned, closing my eyes as I fell backward

onto my bed. For a moment I just lay there, then my eyes snapped open. Slowly, I sat up. "Emily…"

Emily had been the one to tell me about Dad's heart attack. I didn't want to think that way of my sister, but she must have been in on the whole thing. More than angry, it made me feel disappointed in her that she couldn't even trust me to tell me the truth. Then again, her shifty behavior suddenly made much more sense.

"I'm not letting you off the hook so easily, little sister," I muttered to myself, getting up.

I picked up the keys to my car on my way out of the room. I didn't bother taking anything with me just yet because I wasn't sure exactly what my options were. I could always just leave. There was nothing wrong with quitting in the middle, right? Trent did it, even if he did come back. I might even do it if it meant Dad would meet me and explain things to me.

The feeling of betrayal from my sister flared, and with it, indignation. It cooled down almost immediately because no matter what, Emily was my little sister. Hell, I was pretty sure it was Dad who put her up to the whole thing. Emily would never have come up with an idea like that on her own. Dad must have pushed her into it. That made more sense than my sister playing a trick on me with something as serious as a heart attack.

I headed out of the hotel, then bee-lined for the parking lot. I unlocked my car then jumped into the seat.

Several thoughts swirled in my head on the drive back. Why did Emily or Dad feel they'd been pushed to this point? I assumed there was a reason he faked being ill then refused for us to see him. I wasn't sure if I even still wanted to know, considering everything.

Everything was rushing around in my mind like a hurricane and it was making feel as if I was going insane. I needed to calm the fuck down. I couldn't go on like this. I kept thinking about calming down one minute and then the next my anger would boil inside me like hot lava. It was as if I was a volcano ready to explode.

I thought about Laura and her sweet body in my arms and it made me feel whole again. It worked for a while, but then I thought about the way things are between us and I got angry again. I needed to control myself. I pulled my phone out of my pocket and dialed my sister. She picked up quickly.

"Hey, Mason," she chirped. "I'm in the kitchen right now, so can I call you back?"

I could hear some sounds in the background that proved her story, but I wasn't in the mood to be patient. I started to get angry once again, not because of Emily but because of Dad.

"I'm home and I want to see you right now, Emily."

The tone of my voice must have been enough to clue her in that this was something serious because she didn't come back with a refusal. Usually, she'd tell me to wait for her.

"Where are you?" she asked with a sigh.

"I'm at the front door. Just tell me where to meet you and I'll go there. Or you can come pick me up in the foyer."

"It's fine. Just head over to the lounge, all right? I'll be there soon."

I hung up. Though we had more than one lounge in the mansion, besides the large living room we also had, I knew the one she meant. I headed over there, then picked a seat and slumped into it, folding my arms across my chest.

Emily showed up just moments later, and I frowned at her, not bothering to get up to greet her properly. She didn't look like she'd expected it anyway. She had her hands clasped in front of her meekly, her head tilted downward, and an uneasy expression on her face.

"I'm not going to scold you or anything," I said, scowling. "I just wanted to get the news from you directly. I don't know why I had to wait for Trent of all people to tell me about this, Emily."

She had the grace to look contrite, a grimace crossing her face as she took the seat across from me and hesitantly met my gaze.

"Just how mad are you?" she asked.

"Enough to consider tugging your hair right now. I haven't done it since we were kids, but it's not like I won't smack you."

Her eyes widened a bit, and it was almost funny watching her hide her hair with one hand, and her cheek with the other.

I was still too mad to appreciate it.

"I swear it wasn't my idea," she said, shaking her head quickly. "Dad was the one to bring it up, saying something about being lonely. I didn't want to do it, but he was so insistent, and it's Dad, so I couldn't exactly turn him down."

I let out a sigh and she stopped talking immediately.

"I could guess that Dad was the one to put you up to it, Emily, you don't even need to tell me that. I just don't like how you went along with it anyway. Do you have any idea how worried I was? Hell, how worried Trent must have been to come back here? What you both did was so wrong, I don't even know where to begin."

"I know," she said, her voice small. She looked down at her lap, her hair falling over her shoulders to cover the sides of her face. She played with her fingers in her lap, looking every bit the chastened child. "I know I should have done something to stop him from doing something so ridiculous, at least. He did seem to mean it when he said he was lonely, and that he wanted you guys all to come home. Of course, once you all did he couldn't exactly see you…"

No, he couldn't. Not without blowing his cover. Or maybe, he just wanted to prolong the inevitable so we would stick around longer.

"It's okay, Emily," I said, my voice growing softer. "I forgive you for going along with Dad's whims, just promise me you'll never do it again. Dad's a grown up and he should act like it, not put you in awkward situations like this."

"I agreed to it in the end, so it's not like the blame only goes to him, you know. Don't worry. There definitely won't be a second time."

She looked up at me from under her lashes, looking a little hopeful. I sighed, then opened my arms to her. Immediately, she beamed and jumped up, then rushed over to me. She sat down beside me and hugged me from the side, burying her face in my chest. I couldn't help but chuckle because we hadn't been in this position for quite a while.

"I love you, sis," I said, burying my face in her hair. "That won't change just because you make a few stupid choices here and there, but please next time, try to be a little more considerate of other people. Don't just listen and do whatever your old man is telling you to. You're a grown up now."

"I know," she said with a sniff, pulling back, though she was still smiling. "Those days are definitely behind me, I promise."

I wouldn't hold her to that promise, though. Dad could be pretty persuasive when he wanted something.

"I wonder if I should go back to the hotel," I sighed, leaning back against the seat.

"You could always stick around, at least for today?" she suggested. "Mom is around somewhere, and she misses you. Why don't you hang out with us?"

I pursed my lips. "Is Dad around?"

She shrugged. "Nah, I think he headed out at some point to look for Trent over something important. He left a while ago and he hasn't come back yet."

That meant he'd probably gone to the hotel. Which meant, there was no point in me going back there anyway, because I wanted to avoid him for a little bit longer. I could always wait to confront him when he came back.

"All right," I conceded. "I'll stick around." Then I grinned at Emily. "And what is this I hear about you being in the kitchen, huh? Are you still trying to be a chef, or were you lending the staff a hand? Haven't I told you plenty of times about hanging out with the help?"

"But I like it," she said, frowning. "And it's not like I have anything better to do around here. Did you know there was a girl my age working in the kitchen? I had no idea!"

"Imagine what it must be like for her! You're dressed in your usual designer gear and looking like you're about to go to some high-class party. The person who sees that…"

Wasn't going to be particularly happy about it. The truth of my own words hit me. I was pretty much doing what my sister was doing, or at least trying to, and going about it all in the wrong ways. I'd been sending gifts to Laura, expensive shit I thought all women would love, but I forgot I was rubbing our different statuses in her face with such thoughtless gifts.

No wonder they were all returned! I must look like an idiot to take this long just to realize.

Shit!

Would she even let me try to make it up to her?

17

LAURA

I felt weary when I walked into work that day. I knew that another present was waiting for me and I didn't want it. I needed to get him out of my mind but he wasn't going to let it be, so I did the right thing and sent them back. Every single parcel had been returned.

The first gift had come as a surprise. This large, ostentatious display of flowers. There were several roses of exotic colors, and other flowers I didn't even recognize. The humiliating part was receiving it in front of the staff lounge, so plenty of people got to see.

No name came with the gifts, but I knew who they were from. There was only one person I'd been with who had the kind of money to keep buying me things like this.

Mason.

He probably kept his name hidden so the others wouldn't talk. The problem was while they weren't talking about Mason, they sure talked plenty about me and how lucky I was to have seduced some rich guy.

As if!

I didn't know why he was so interested in me. I'd figured the one night between us would have been enough. He didn't seek me out for a while, and I assumed everything was okay, but then the gifts started, and I wondered if avoiding him pushed him to try this.

After the initial surprise of the gifts and me sending them back, I hadn't known how to feel. There was anger, resentment, all sorts of negative emotions whirling in my chest once I realized that this was his new tactic to try and get me to see him. Above everything else was a disappointment. One minute I felt as if I was getting to know him and that the relationship I'd never envisaged having was slowly becoming my reality.

There was one question that kept entering my mind, how did Mason see me?

It had plagued my mind, almost become an obsession like Mason sending the gifts. It shouldn't matter, considering we were nothing to each other anymore. I couldn't help letting it get to me. It had taken some time for me to work through my feelings after that first gift, and in the end, I'd locked myself up in a bathroom and cried my eyes out for half an hour before going back to work.

Ever since that first time, every single darn time I received one of those gifts, I would break down and cry again.

It had been a week and I was tired of crying. I was also getting sick of the rumors flying around. I didn't snag some rich guy. It was just a spoiled child who probably saw me as one of his toys that wanted to get away, and he was doing this to try and stop that from happening. If anything, it just cemented the fact we really couldn't be in a relationship together. I wouldn't accept even a fling. Because that just wasn't me.

Not that I would ever let the bastard know just to what extent he could affect me, that he could bring me to tears with an expensive gift.

I'd never asked him for one anyway, so why was he sending them? It was a poor choice if he thought it would change my mind. If he'd clued into the fact I was avoiding him, he could have just respected that.

He probably didn't even know how his treatment seemed to outsiders. I mean, I was a maid, and I'd always grown up not having much. What did he expect, that I would wear designer clothes as I walked down the street? I wasn't nearly so ashamed of myself that I thought I needed a wardrobe change. I couldn't wear the expensive jewelry he sent me while working. That would only lead to stares and questions I'd rather avoid. And the candy… for the sake of my health, I couldn't eat it. And just seeing them so intricately packaged, I could only guess at the price and the lavish tastes, they didn't suit me even if I did eat them.

Mason was treating me like his mistress. I wasn't some man's trinket. I was a human being, with thoughts and emotions; not someone who'd fall all over a man for expensive gifts. I was pretty minimalistic. I'd always lived on a budget and I didn't see any shame in it. It was my life, after all.

I didn't wear a lot of jewelry to begin with, not unless I

had a date, and then it would be a simple pair of earrings and a necklace, maybe a bracelet and some rings. I had quite a few, and all of them had been left to me by my mother. I was lucky enough not to have lost them with all the foster houses I'd been through, and I treasured them too much to replace them with anything else, even if that 'anything else' probably cost way more than my entire jewelry collection.

I didn't collect trinkets like the starlets he was probably used to having on his arm and inviting to his parties. They might appreciate receiving something from him, but if it wasn't something I could reciprocate, then it was going to make me feel uncomfortable. No matter how young, good-looking and rich he was, I wasn't going to stand for being treated like one of his conquests either.

Thankfully, when I made it into the staff room, there wasn't anyone waiting for me to come in to deliver some new gift. There were plenty of staff milling around just watching the door like they wanted to check out what else was coming, as if it was any of their business. I understood how sensational it was for them though. Nothing like this ever happened in the time since I'd worked at the hotel. I wanted to crawl under the table just to escape their stares, but then I saw an inviting face and immediately felt some relief.

"Jessi!" I hurried to join her on the seat, sticking close to her side for moral support.

"Hey, Laura," she said, keeping her voice casual, and even throwing an arm around my shoulders to pull me closer. I shot my friend a grateful smile. "Thank goodness you came early. I was worried you'd get here late and your drink would already have cooled down by then."

I looked at the table in front of us, and for the first time noticed that there were two mugs on it and a plate of pastries. I reached for one, feeling grateful my friend was a really good pastry chef. We dug in, and I felt just a little lighter because of it.

"Do you mind telling me what's going on?" she asked, keeping her voice low.

Thankfully, there hadn't been any gifts coming in, and before it got too late to clock into work, other staff started disappearing and going to their jobs. I still had some time left, and I couldn't help but sigh as I noticed the room was nearly empty.

"I want to, but I'm not sure if I should," I said honestly, hesitating to open up but feeling the need to confide in Jessi. She was my best friend. She was the right person to talk to, especially because I hadn't been honest with her about Mason.

She arched an eyebrow. "You've got a man..." She paused waiting for a reaction from me. "Someone that keeps sending you these gifts..."

"There wasn't one today," I said, feeling hopeful. "I just hope he finally got the message," I said with relief and disappointment at the same time.

She nodded with a quirk of the lips. "Yeah. Only during the holidays or your birthday, and only if you get to respond in kind. You refused some of my presents when I gave them to you. Do you remember?"

"You give me treats plenty of times and I eat those," I pointed out. "So what exactly are you upset about?"

"I'm not upset about anything. Just I know I kept things from you when I was having issues with Trent, and I will respect your decision if you decide to do the same, but..."

"I know," I said, bumping my shoulder against hers lightly. "You're here to listen to me if I want to talk about it. I offered you the same thing, remember? I just... don't think I want to."

"Because you can't talk about it?" she asked.

I shook my head. "Because I just want to forget it. It... was a moment of weakness for me. While I couldn't call it a mistake, it's not something I plan on repeating, either."

She nodded in understanding. "Whoever it is, they seem pretty determined to get you back."

I snorted and rolled my eyes. "That bastard can just go and throw himself off a cliff if he thinks this is the way to go about it. Expensive candy and delicate gold bracelets... I'm not the kind of woman to be bought by that kind of stuff."

"I know you're not," she said, soothing, patting a hand down my back. "Here, why don't you finish up and we can both get to work before we're late, hmm?"

I did as she asked, picking up another pastry and biting into it, then bringing the sweet mocha drink to my lips for a sip. It was a little too much sweets, but I figured I deserved something like this. Besides, while Jessi didn't know about the whole cancer thing, she knew how careful I was about my health and my diet. She was doing this as a pick me up, and she hadn't tried to get me to test taste anything for her for a few days.

"We better head out," she said once we had everything done. We took the dishes to the kitchen, where she caught me by surprise as she pulled me into a quick hug. "Hang in there, okay? I'll talk to you again after work."

"Thanks for being such a good friend, Jessi," I said simply.

She smiled at me, then went off. I did the same before changing in the nearly empty lockers. Nothing else had come, and I hoped it was the end of those presents and Mason seeking me out. If he'd kept it up, I would have gone to look for him myself just to get him to stop, because I wouldn't have him thinking any of this would win me over.

I managed to get through work without any incidents, and at the end of the day, I felt relieved when I got home. For the first time in a while, I thought I could relax, and went to get out my knitting. I hadn't sat down for long, though, when there was a knock on my door.

Putting my knitting aside, I went to see who it was. I didn't usually get visitors, so I was curious. I opened the door, and my jaw dropped.

Mason was standing at my doorstep. Great, he didn't send a gift this time, just himself. I didn't know whether to laugh or cry. I'd missed him, but I had to think of myself and that meant keeping him as far away from me as possible, It was going to be hard.

18

LAURA

"How did you know where I live?" I asked, my voice quivering. I was scared, not about him coming to see me, but about what was going to happen next. Mason adopted this sheepish look.

"I swear I'm not trying to be a stalker, or anything," he said quickly, then winced as if he realized the admission wasn't making anything better.

"Seriously, how did you know?"

"I didn't use the employee records or anything. I asked someone at the hotel and they told me. I wasn't sure what time you'd be back, but I wanted to at least try." There was desperation in his voice.

Did I really mean that much to him?

Was I really just being paranoid?

If he'd gone through my records at the hotel, he would have crossed a line. I wondered who told him where I lived, and if they'd find it strange I had someone sending me expensive gifts and one of the boss's sons asking after me. I could only hope no one would make the connection and spread more rumors. I had enough shit to deal with as it was.

"Can we talk? I've been trying to find you for some time now—"

"No," I said abruptly. "I'm going to respectfully decline and ask that you go away and stop sending me things, Mason."

His expression betrayed surprise for a moment before he was able to mask it.

"Why exactly won't you see me?" he asked with a slight frown on his face. "This isn't going according to plan. I thought that you would be happy to see me. Happy to receive the gifts, not just send them back. I don't get it. Is there something wrong with me that means you can't see me?"

When he said it like that, I felt kind of ashamed of myself. Yes, I knew how my actions looked, but to have him say it so bluntly… It was like I'd used him knowingly, only to throw him aside. And I couldn't even say that wasn't true because in a lot of ways it was. I'd been down that day, and I'd taken his hand because it was something I wanted without thinking about the consequences. And then immediately afterward I'd tried to put a wall between us.

"I'm sorry that things turned out this way. I swear it's not what I planned, but Mason you do understand that this can't go anywhere, right? If it's a fling you want, I'm sure there are other women you could go for other than me."

"I want you!" he said stubbornly.

My heart, traitorous thing that it was, skipped a beat at the bold declaration. I could feel some heat in my cheeks, but I tried not to let myself be swayed. No matter what he said, I'd made my decision already. The week of careless gifts he'd been sending me cemented that this was the right thing to do.

"Mason, please," I said with a sigh, leaning against the doorjamb. "You're young, you're hot. Not only can you do better, I'm sure there are plenty of women that would fall all over you if they thought they had a chance with you."

"That's rich coming from you. You did the complete opposite," he said.

I narrowed my eyes. "Seriously, kid. Go away. I didn't fall all over you because I'm not that kind of woman to begin with, so I don't know what you were hoping for by sending me all those things. I'm not the kind of person who can be bought, and I don't need a man who thinks that way. You have a million women waiting for the opportunity to be chosen by you, so don't come to me anymore—"

"What the hell! Don't call me kid!" he said.

I snorted. "Mason, I do happen to know your real age, you know. When I first met you a few years ago, you were just barely legal."

"I was nineteen," he cut in.

"Like I said, barely legal." I frowned after I said it. He remembered me, even that far back? I shook the thought off, reminding myself once again not to be swayed.

"Is the age difference really a big deal?" he asked.

"There are so many problems, Mason, I don't even have time to worry about the age difference."

Not that I didn't worry about it. While I hadn't paid much attention to him in the first few years, I did definitely look when he was twenty-one, and I kept looking after that. Mostly, it was because it was around that time he'd had his first racy party and stripped down. The first time us maids realized that this kid was going to be a recurring problem if he stuck around.

It still felt like robbing the cradle just being near this guy and allowing his interest in me to continue.

"What if I said your age didn't matter to me?" he asked. "Because it really doesn't. It definitely doesn't change how I see you—"

"And how exactly do you see me?" I countered, tilting my chin up. "Explain it to me, Mason, how exactly do you see me that you thought sending me all that stuff was okay? And sending it to me at work! If you knew my home address, then I wouldn't have minded them coming here but I would still have sent them back. The real problem is you had them sent to my work where people would notice and talk! What were you thinking?"

"I only found out where you live yesterday, I didn't know your address a week ago, or I would have brought the presents here myself."

"Well then, I'm sad now that you didn't. My week would have gone a lot better if I could have shut this idea down earlier."

Mason frowned in obvious displeasure. This wasn't going as he must have hoped it would. He must have thought it would be easy. I'd pegged him early on as the kind of man who got whatever he wanted, spoiled by his parents. That wasn't the kind of person I wanted to try dating.

"I didn't mean for things to get out of hand. It's just… you were avoiding me, and I didn't know how else to see you. I also didn't know what to do to get you talking to me, so I started sending the presents. I know it was stupid for it to take me a week to realize why you returned everything, but I think I understand now."

I narrowed my eyes, wondering exactly what it was that this kid thought he understood. If he really had, he wouldn't be at my front door like this.

"Look, kid—"

"I'm serious, Laura. Stop with the kid stuff, it's freaking me out," he said, frowning a little. "I acknowledge that there's a gap between us. But I've been an adult for a while now, you know?"

I bit my lip, feeling my heart react to his words and his serious tone. He was right, and I knew it. No matter how spoiled he might be, Mason was every bit a man. I kept trying to refer to him as a kid hoping it could create some space between us.

That was probably unfair of me. He was right, treating him like a kid when he clearly wasn't was a little degrading. I hadn't liked it when older people had treated me the same back when I was in college. In fact, Mason was more mature than I was at that age, and I had to respect that.

"Fine," I said with a sigh. "Look, Mason. I don't know what exactly it is that you want from me, but I'll tell you right now that you won't get it. Yes, we had sex once. It was nice." I chose the word deliberately, feeling a bit of shame because I'd just thought it would be disrespectful to call him a kid. I definitely felt a zing of pleasure when my 'nice' caused his face to fall, because he needed to be knocked down a peg or two. "We had our night and it ended, and it's time to move on now. You understand, don't you?"

"No, I don't," he said, his frown deepening, and he sounded a little hurt. "I don't understand, Laura. Why don't you try explaining things in more detail for me, hmm?"

"Don't make this difficult for me, please. I have a life, so do you, so why can't we go back to it? I'm not asking that you forget anything happened, just think of it as one moment in your life that is now gone, and we can both move on. I already have a date tonight," I added, fibbing, but he didn't need to know that. "I just got back home and I wanted to relax a little and shower before he showed up. It'll look bad if he comes and you're still standing here."

Mason was scowling at me now, but I didn't even feel bad for the lie. I didn't want to be cruel, because even if he was a man and considered himself one, he was still young. His personality was still annoying, but it wouldn't be fair of me to keep resenting him for his birth as if it was his fault he was so rich. He didn't ask for his lot in life any more than I did.

For a long moment, he didn't say anything, and I grew nervous the longer he stayed silent. I couldn't read his expression. I didn't know what he was thinking, and that had me unsettled. He wasn't leaving either, and I wondered if he was going to keep trying to talk me into dating him.

I wanted him to just leave! As early as possible, so I wouldn't have the opportunity to waver. Already, I'd felt it in my chest when my heart beat at his words, and I didn't want to be swayed when I'd already chosen this path for myself. He should have respected that and walked away, but I wondered if he knew I wasn't being entirely truthful, or if it was just his ego keeping him in place.

As I watched, this determined expression took over his face, and it was enough to have me backing up. My arms crossed over my chest, and while I could have just walked into my apartment and closed the door on his face, the look in his eyes kept me still.

He had a basket in his hands I'd only just noticed. My eyes didn't stay away from his face for long, and I could see a look of confidence in his gaze like he knew just what he had to do now, and I wondered to what extent he had read me. I braced myself for whatever he had to say to me, already knowing it was going to be torture to turn him down.

19

MASON

"Laura. Do you really have a date for tonight?"

I asked, because while it surprised me when she said it, it also struck me as odd. I didn't know much about her, and what I'd heard about her probably wasn't enough to base anything on. While her gaze had remained steady on mine up to the end of our little conversation, there were moments when she'd seemed a little off.

I was the deal maker of the family and it involved knowing how to read people well. I hadn't even tried before with Laura, besides seeing her obvious attraction to me, and that was another mistake I'd made.

This time, I was going to do things properly, and I wasn't going to let her just run away from me without a fight.

"So what if I do?" she countered after a moment of floundering, her chin tilting up higher. "Whether I do or not, it's not any of your business, is it?"

"Now, who's acting like a kid? True, if you do it has nothing to do with me. But that poor guy is just wasting his time. He doesn't have a chance with you," I said, folding my arms.

She let out a small huff. "Aren't you being just a little conceited right now?"

I shook my head. "I wouldn't say that. If anything, you could say I have some confidence. Because you can try to hide it all you want, Laura, but I can tell you want me. You wouldn't have taken my hand that night if you didn't; if all you really wanted was one night. You're right, that's not the kind of person you are. I'm sorry for not seeing it before but I definitely see it now."

Her eyes widened in surprise, her expression going slightly dazed. A second later, she rearranged her expression, though it looked like she was having some trouble. Her eyes wavered once more before meeting mine again, and I would have smiled in triumph but I didn't want her to see it and pull back.

"How smooth," she muttered. "I can see why women fall for you. Even with everything else, you have enough charm to make any woman do whatever you want them to do. Don't you?"

I chuckled. "I don't see it that way. There are things you're born with and things you can do on your own. My charm is something I perfected all by myself."

After all, I'd done a great job keeping my hidden emotions from all my family and friends over the years. No one had ever seen me lose control, unless it was of the drunk variety, because I never let them see it. Instead I watched people, found ways to keep them fooled, learned to read them all like open books. Back when I was a teenager, even when I was part of my high school rugby team, I'd always thought it was me against the world. That mentality had made it slightly easier to quit the game when Dad made me do it.

"Just because you have a little charm, it doesn't mean I'm going to be all over you, you know," she blustered.

I noticed how she tensed her arms around herself and pressed her lips together. I was affecting her and she didn't like it. She was probably telling herself something along the lines of 'don't be swayed'. While I couldn't say she was like any woman I'd met before, Laura was still a woman, after all.

"I brought you something," I said, raising the basket up.

Her eyes were curious, but in the next second, she narrowed them and looked up at me with a scowl.

"You haven't had enough of me returning your gifts? Do I have to do it personally for you to get it?"

"I'm hoping you'll accept this one. Especially because it was hand delivered," I said honestly. "I was careless before but I put some thought into this, so I hope you'll think about accepting it."

She was still frowning, but the curiosity was back in her face as she looked down at the basket. She even uncrossed her arms, meaning she wasn't on the defensive as much. I was being insistent, and it was probably annoying for her. I didn't want to give up though, and not just for the sake of my pride. I actually wanted something with Laura, and I knew it would be an uphill battle, but I no longer cared.

"What is it?" she asked, peering closer.

The fact she wanted to know what was in the basket, let me know that all things were not lost. With a smile, I held the basket out to her, so she could take a look. She did so cautiously at first, then her eyes went wide again as her mouth parted.

"This is all..."

"Groceries," I finished for her. "Hopefully, things you like. I asked around a bit for healthy food. I hoped you'd at least appreciate this. And if you're worried about reciprocating, though it's really not necessary, I won't mind you making dinner for me some time. It would only be fair, after all, since I did cook you steak last time."

She looked up at me.

"Why are you so shocked?" I teased.

"It's just... so thoughtful of you..."

"And you didn't expect that of me?"

"What?" she said, blinking. "Oh! No, no. That isn't what I meant, it's just..."

Her voice trailed off like she couldn't come up with a real refusal. I chuckled because this was the first time I was seeing her act so cute. There were many sides to Laura, and I wanted to know them all.

"There's also some prepared food in there," I added. "The dishes are down in the bottom; I was hoping to keep them warm on the way here. It's not bought at a restaurant or anything. I was home earlier, and I helped my sister to cook everything. Mom even joined in but I did most of the work."

I wasn't even bragging. Whatever Emily had been doing

in the kitchen before I arrived, I offered to help her cook instead of making the staff do it. She'd pretty much had me do everything. Mom, who we'd spent the afternoon with, had joined in too. They both got a kick out of watching me cook for them and had hung back as much as I'd allowed them.

"What is it?" Laura asked.

"Why don't you let me inside and I'll show you?"

She bit down on her lip. I wasn't about to let her back away though, and I lowered the basket to my side, taking a step closer to her and leaning my head down a little. She watched me, and I was grateful when she didn't try to back away.

"Laura," I said, my voice going a little husky. I couldn't help it with the proximity to her. "Can I please come in?"

She looked like she was considering it. A wave of relief went through my chest, and I was a little awed at the feeling. If she'd turned me down flat, it would have bothered me. Relief wasn't something I often felt when it came to women outside of my family unless it was someone clingy finally deciding to let go.

"The food is getting cold," I prompted. "And I cooked it especially for you. At least tell me what you think of it."

That seemed to make her cave, and my lips twitched. She hadn't said the words yet, I couldn't smile just yet.

"Okay," she said, finally, after another minute. She stepped aside to let me go through. "I haven't started on food yet, so I hope you have something good in there."

I didn't know her tastes but I hoped she'd like it. I at least knew she liked to eat healthily, and I'd thought to ask one of the cooks at the mansion instead of depending on the Internet for ideas.

Her apartment was so small it was like a little box. My hotel suite probably had bigger space. There was a couch, a single seat, a coffee table, and a couple of stools. There were some knickknacks piled in one corner I didn't look particularly close at.

Even as small as it was, she kept the place clean, if a little cluttered. There were plenty of bright, vibrant colors all over the room, nothing like my stark white hotel room, or the marble foyer in the mansion. I could tell by just looking around that the place was lived in.

"Follow me," she said, taking the lead. "The kitchen is this way."

I could have made it on my own. In the tiny room, there was one door, and one open archway, and it was easy to guess which would lead to the bedroom, which to the kitchen. Still, I followed dutifully behind her.

"Tell me if there's something you don't like," I said. "I'll take it back and replace it with something else."

"You don't have to get me anymore," she said, frowning at me. Then her expression softened. "Thank you. It's a thoughtful gift. And I'll admit, I didn't think you had it in you."

I didn't even care she was technically insulting me. I was just glad she was no longer pushing me away, and I smiled with just a hint of pride showing.

We put the groceries away in her kitchen, then I got the food out. She looked especially curious when I opened three different dishes.

"What is all this?" she asked.

"Well, I thought chicken salad since we had steak last time. I thought about making fish, but I don't like packing fish, it's best eaten right away. You'll probably want to warm this. There's also steamed veggies with a Greek yogurt sauce, and the last dish is a fruit salad with honey orange glaze. It's been a while since I've cooked anything so fancy, but my family liked it, so I hope you do too."

We heated everything up, then sat down at her tiny dinner table to eat. I waited to see her reaction to everything before I ate it myself. She seemed to like all of it, and I felt another wave of relief. I watched her eat happily, almost forgetting to get in some bites myself.

In that moment, all I cared about was that Laura was happy.

20

MASON

Once we were done eating, I followed Laura back to the kitchen to clean everything up. She was insistent on me returning with the empty dishes and the basket, even though I didn't have to. When she nearly pushed it all into my arms, I folded them over my chest.

"I feed you and now you want to kick me out? Great!" I teased with a cheeky grin.

She took me seriously and looked flustered as she set the basket down on the counter.

"Well, you just came to eat dinner with me, right? The dinner you made for me. It was all very good, thank you, but won't your family be wondering where you are?"

I shook my head. "No. I'm not staying at the mansion. I just went there today because I was free from work and I wanted to visit."

Technically, I'd skipped out on work. And I'd forgotten to ask why Trent was still around considering Dad had tricked us into coming back, he knew and was still here.

Dad had gone to see him, and I wondered what they'd talked about. He hadn't arrived home by the time I wanted to leave, so I was putting off speaking to him for something much more important.

"Didn't they wonder why you took all that food with you?"

"Not really. They already know I'm living alone at the hotel, and while they do trust the hotel's standards, Mom was happy to see me take home food she'd helped to make. They probably figured I'd eat the leftovers tomorrow or something. They didn't even ask."

"And the groceries?"

"I went to the supermarket nearby and bought them. It's the first time I've ever done that," I admitted.

"Going to a supermarket?" she asked.

I shrugged. "You can have just about everything delivered to your doorstep these days, even groceries. It was… a strange experience?"

I couldn't exactly decide what I'd thought of it. I'd of course seen grocery stores on TV. I'd known what to expect, sort of. Still, I left home early to go and shop with the list I'd made up. Laura smiled, seeming amused.

"Everything I bought should be useful to you. If you'd like, I could lend you some nice recipes. It's all either stuff I've eaten or something that's been recommended to me."

"What would you have done if I hadn't taken your gift?" she asked, curious.

I shrugged and said, "I would have taken it all to the hotel with me. You know my room has a kitchen. I've been known to use it once or twice for more than just beer storage."

She wasn't trying to push me to go, and I let a small smile cross my lips, satisfied I'd sufficiently distracted her. But then, I found myself distracted as well as I looked at her. When she smiled, it lit up her whole face. The effect was especially beautiful compared to how she'd looked when she was scowling at me, trying to get me to leave.

My body moved on its own, closing the space between us as my hand rose to her cheek. The smile dropped when she saw just how close I was getting. She eyed my hand as I brought it to her face, but she didn't flinch or try to avoid me, and I took it as a good sign. I leaned down, moving my face a little closer to hers.

"Laura," I murmured. "You never did answer my question before."

"What question?" she breathed out.

"Are you trying to kick me out? Do you want me to leave?"

I'd imposed on her enough. No matter how much more I wanted, she'd let me in figuratively and literally. If she asked me to leave again, I definitely would because I didn't want to risk getting on her bad side again.

She didn't say anything immediately, and it gave me hope.

"Laura…"

"Stay," she said before I could ask again.

That made me grin. Then I leaned my head down a little more and lightly pressed my lips against hers.

We were both still. I couldn't even say it was a kiss, even

a chaste one, it was just a press of lips. I didn't know if I should continue or not because while she'd asked me to stay, I wanted her to participate, not just go along with this because I wanted it. So, when she sighed into the kiss and pressed a little closer, her body coming into contact with mine, I let myself relax.

Carefully, I moved my lips against hers, pushing just a little closer. Laura placed her hands on my chest, and I lowered both of mine to wrap my arms around her waist.

I wanted to give her the whole soft and romantic routine, but dammit, I was a man and holding back completely wasn't easy for me. So after a moment of careful, closed-mouth kissing that felt unnecessarily long, I licked and nipped at her bottom lip until she parted them for me. I slid my tongue into her mouth, groaning as I backed her slowly against the counter. She moved with me, clearly wanting this as much as I did.

When I pulled back from the kiss, we were both panting for breath, and our eyes met for a short moment.

"I want you," I admitted.

"Me too," she said, breathless.

That was all the encouragement I needed. I moved back just far enough to see what I was doing and lifted her shirt. She raised her arms so I could pull it off her, and the top she had on underneath it went next.

My lips dropped to her neck as I made my way down, cupping her breasts and massaging them gently through her bra. When my mouth reached the top of her bra, I reached an arm around her to undo the clasp.

A hand on my chest stopped me, and I froze, looking up at her. Did she want me to stop?

"Can we move to the bedroom?" Laura asked, her chest rising up and down with her quickened breaths, lips parted and glistening, eyes burning with heat.

Relief, followed quickly by desire, filled my chest. I nodded as I moved back.

"Lead the way."

She bit her lip, my eyes following the movement. She crouched down to pick up her dropped clothes, then took my hand and led me to the other door in the room. She hit a switch against the wall, and the lights came on. It wasn't necessary, but it was good because I wanted to see her.

Before she could turn around, I slid my arms around her waist and pulled her back against me. She let out a gasp when her ass met my groin, and I smirked.

"Be patient," I murmured, leaning down to place kisses all over her neck. "We'll get there soon enough."

"Shut up," she muttered, sounding a little embarrassed.

I didn't get a chance to say anything more before she did something to stun me into silence. With her hands over mine, she guided them up her stomach, to her breasts, and squeezed. She moaned, tilting her head back against my shoulder, and my eyes dropped to her closed eyes and parted mouth, the line of her neck. I saw over her shoulder where both our hands were cupping her breasts, and the visual had my cock throbbing in my briefs.

Yeah, having the light on was a good plan.

After one last peck on her neck, I pulled my hands out from under hers to turn her around, all my patience gone. I took a look around and noticed how this room was way smaller than the living room. The bed took up most of the space. This was an apartment meant for one person, though two could probably live comfortably enough.

The bed was a little small, but if we squeezed close, I thought it could work. That idea had me grinning, and I backed Laura toward the bed until she sat back on it.

"What has you so happy?" she asked.

"Your bed is small," I said with a shrug.

I reached around her to unclasp her bra, and this time she didn't stop me. I eased the straps off her arms, and let the bra fall to the floor. I had just a tad more patience than last time, and I wasn't intoxicated, so I got a good look at her. I must have stayed still for too long because she started squirming.

"Why does my bed being small making you happy?" she asked.

"Because it means we're going to be close tonight."

I didn't give her a chance to reply, swooping in with a long, wet kiss just long enough to keep her distracted. My hands went for the waistband of her pants, and she fell back onto the bed as I pulled them off, leaving her in only her panties. She squirmed higher up the bed, and I took off my shirt and pants before following her, crawling above her on all fours.

"My bed isn't as soft as yours," she warned.

I shrugged. "Not a problem. I've slept in rougher places than you'd think."

There was skepticism on her face, but I didn't care. It wasn't like I was going to give her any details though. Most of them were stories best left in the past for security reasons.

I lowered myself over her carefully, then took her lips in a kiss. She kissed me back, her hands roaming all over my body, going around my waist to feel out my back. One of her legs wrapped around my waist, and when I rocked my hips down, we both groaned out. She was warm and wet through her panties, and we were both done waiting as we stripped each other bare.

Laura pulled me on top of her once again, both her legs wrapping around me as I wrapped my arms around her back. With a bit of shifting, the head of my cock touched her entrance, and as she moved her hips up and I rocked down, I entered her in one smooth thrust, eyes closed, and head thrown back in pleasure.

I forced them back open in a moment, looking down at Laura. Her own eyes were closed, and her mouth was opened as she panted for breath. I started to move my hips, slowly, carefully. Every movement was calculated to give her the most pleasure. This wasn't just us fucking again. This was me making this woman mine in the best way. Gently, but with obvious passion. Her nails dug into my back as I rolled my hips, and I hissed.

My lips found hers as our bodies continued to rock together. I picked up a rhythm, moving just a little bit faster, occasionally adding a roll and a twist to my hips to hit all her pleasure spots.

This is what life can be when done right, I told her silently, with every movement, and she responded beautifully to each one. I was addicted to the sweet sounds falling out of her lips, deep moans, soft gasps, and delicate whimpers. I never wanted the moment to end, I wanted to hear them more.

I groaned as my body shook in an orgasm, and Laura let out a cry as she trembled in my arms.

Afterward, I rolled us over with her still in my arms and my cock still inside her, pulling her body close to mine. I was sated, but even as Laura dozed in my arms, I didn't feel tired.

I'm in trouble, I thought to myself.

This was something new to me, so I thought I might have been mistaken, but I knew it now. Laura was in my blood. She wasn't just some fuck to me, what we just did was making love.

The real problem was I didn't want to ever get her out.

21

MASON

I woke up feeling so peaceful. It was as if I was having an out of body experience because I'd never felt this way before. It was an unusual enough occurrence that I opened my eyes with a frown instead of a smile, only for one to appear anyway as I looked at the body cuddled into my chest.

The bed was tiny, too small for both of us to be lying on our backs side by side and still fit, considering how broad my shoulders were. There was also the matter of height because my feet were just a bit further than the end of the bed. I'd insisted on us sleeping like this, with me holding her and our legs tangled so it would be more comfortable for us both.

I could have slept on the floor without any trouble, as long as she didn't try to make me leave, because I didn't want to leave her.

"Laura," I whispered, placing a kiss on her bare shoulder.

A small frown appeared on her face, and she squirmed in my arms. I moaned a little as we pressed close together, and I could feel every movement of her body against mine. Her soft breasts pressed against my chest, her soft curves… my cock hardened against her stomach as she frowned and squirmed some more.

"You didn't forget I stayed over, did you?" I asked teasingly, not sure whether or not she was awake enough to hear me. "Because that would be awkward once you open your eyes."

I wondered if she'd heard me, but then a moment later, she opened her eyes. She squinted up at me, and I tensed, wondering if she'd kick me out. Then she smiled sleepily, and I swore my heart skipped a beat.

"Hey," she said, her voice hoarse. "You're still here."

I arched an eyebrow. "Did you think I would leave in the middle of the night or something? I have no intention of doing that."

Her smile took on a sheepish edge. "Sorry."

I rolled my eyes. If she was apologizing for leaving me after our first night together now, it was a little late for it.

"It's fine," I said, then leaned down for a kiss.

"I haven't brushed my teeth," she complained, leaning her head back.

I grinned. "Neither have I."

She didn't get a chance to voice another complaint before I leaned down to press a quick kiss to her lips. She blinked up at me, then wrapped her arms around my neck to drag me down for a longer kiss. After long moments of just making out, I rolled us over, Laura's legs parting naturally to fit me between them. My now fully hard cock rubbed against her stomach, and I shuddered at the feeling.

We both shifted, hands roaming each other's bodies, rocking and rolling gently together. With a shift of my hips, the head of my cock was at her entrance, and I slid inside her. I thrust gently against her, with my hand on her hip, urging her to follow my lead.

I placed kisses all over her skin, wherever I could reach; her face, neck, shoulders, chest. I could tell she was close to coming because her breathing changed. I moved slightly faster as she let out a gasp at the end of every breath. She whimpered as her walls convulsed around my cock, and I groaned as my body stilled and shuddered in an orgasm.

I rolled off her, pulling her on top of my chest as we both caught our breath. I blinked lazily at the early morning light filtering in through the curtain. I wondered what time it was.

"Do you have to go into work today?" I asked, hoping that she didn't have to go, but then feeling selfish about wanting her all to myself. "I don't want to make you late."

She didn't seem to be in a hurry, though, yawning as she stretched her body on top of mine.

"Nah, it's fine. It's my day off today, so I don't have to go anywhere."

I relaxed into the bed, closing my eyes for a moment, one of my hands running up and down Laura's back.

There was something I'd forgotten about. I still had to take care of the family matter, and I probably had to get it out of the way soon. I had Laura now, so I didn't think I'd just leave town immediately.

"Breakfast?" I offered, opening my eyes and looking down at the woman lying drowsily on my chest. Shit, what had got into me? I would never feel emotional with a woman before; usually it was in and out as fast as my cock died down, but now I just wanted to stay. Not to fuck or do anything, but to have her company.

Her eyes opened into slits and she considered me silently, before rolling off me. I took that as silent agreement and got out of bed. I picked my clothes up from the floor and put them on, then left her with a peck on the forehead, going to the kitchen.

I picked out some of the stuff I'd brought over last night and used it to make something light. I hummed as I worked, and I heard over my cooking when Laura went to take a shower.

By the time she showed up to the kitchen, dressed in tights and a large jumper that fell to the tops of her thighs, I was setting two plates on the table.

"This looks good," she said, taking the other seat once I sat down.

"Sorry, I think I used your last eggs. I'll get more later."

"It's fine," she said quickly, shaking her head.

I watched as she picked up her fork and popped some food in her mouth. She chewed thoughtfully, then smiled.

"Hey, this is good."

"I told you I'm not just good looking, I'm pretty good in the kitchen too."

I was being arrogant. Maybe there was still a part of me that was still real.

"I'm not used to vegetables in my eggs," she said, and I

could tell by the expression on her face that she was thinking that she wasn't going to enjoy them. She was going to fucking love them. Don't judge a book by its cover! That was my motto and as soon as she tried it, she'd regret her comment.

"I fried some vegetables and added a little bit of fruit, a tiny bit of salt and the egg on top. It's a pretty easy recipe."

"You seem to have a lot of those," she said. "I'm wondering if you just borrowed them all from somewhere."

"I've moved around a bit, so you could say I've been exposed to different tastes and cuisines. Basically, I try to remake what I liked. A lot of it is from home though," I admitted and wondered whether to tell her about my travels and about studying in England. But then something stopped me from saying anything else. Maybe because a part of me knew that Laura and I hadn't had the same experiences and I didn't want her to think that I was showing off. So I kept quiet.

We ate silently, then I got up to clean the dishes before she could. Once I was done, I turned to lean against the counter, facing her.

"I think maybe we can talk now?" I asked.

That had her perking up, straightening her spine, her expression taking an uneasy cast.

I chuckled. "Why do you look like that? It's only fair, isn't it? I've wanted to talk to you for a while but you kept avoiding me."

"What could we possibly have to talk about?" she asked, narrowing her eyes as her lips pursed.

I picked the chair across from her at the table and moved it, so it was closer to her, facing her directly. I sat down on it, leaning forward so our faces were close.

"I'm going to ask you a question, and I need you to answer me honestly, Laura. Do you or do you not like me? If you tell me right now that you don't like me, whether you mean it or not, I will take you seriously and leave you alone after today."

My heart was beating fast in my chest because I felt uneasy. I didn't want her to say it. Especially if she didn't mean it, because I would have to walk away. However, I knew we wouldn't be getting anywhere if all I did was keep chasing her when she was insistent on running away from me. As much as it could be a fun sort of a challenge, I didn't want to see her that way. I didn't want my relationship with Laura to be like that.

I wanted a real relationship with her, another first for me because while I'd had flings, I'd never had a girlfriend before. But this was Laura, and I thought she could be the one, the woman I could commit to.

After a long moment, where I thought I wouldn't be able to hold out my impatience, she reacted. She let out a heavy sigh as she leaned back in her chair, her head rolled to the side to meet my gaze.

"It's not as simple as that," she said, a little frown on her face. "I don't think this is a good idea, but I don't want to never see you again. When I was avoiding you before... I did it because I thought it was for the best, but I missed you too."

I could imagine how difficult it was for her to admit

that much, her hesitation was too long for it to have been an easy decision to make. But I was happy she'd admitted it to me and to herself.

"Can we just try and have a relationship without you thinking about all the reasons why we shouldn't be together?" I asked. "That's all I'm really asking for. I mean, I've never dated myself, but if we try…"

"You've never dated before?" she asked, incredulous.

I shook my head with a chuckle. "No, not like long-term dating anyway. Not even in high school. You could say I… have a problem with trusting people. Outside of family, I can't say I've ever really trusted anybody."

"And you trust me?" she asked, eyebrow arched.

"I can't explain it, but I feel like I can so I do. You never have to try to avoid me or run away from me again. I know I tend to be insistent and it can get annoying, but I won't ever disregard anything you say. If later you tell me you want to break up… well, I'll try to change your mind probably, but I'll respect it."

It was probably more than I'd ever spoken honestly to any woman I'd ever been with. Laura didn't reply, her expression complicated.

"Let me try," I said quietly. "I know we're different, but I want to show you I do know what life is about, even if I do seem like some spoiled rich brat at times."

Her face warmed, and she stood abruptly from the chair, taking some steps away from me. She couldn't meet my gaze but I held my breath as I waited for her reply.

"Alright," she said, her voice even quieter than mine. I might have missed it if I wasn't listening so intently. Before

I could say anything, though, she turned around and rushed out of the kitchen, calling over her shoulder. "I need to go change!"

I couldn't help but grin, watching her rush off. I wanted to know what was going through her head that made her retreat with a burning face, but she was cute, so I didn't mind.

I had what I wanted now—a chance with Laura. All I had to do was not blow it, because she was exactly what I needed right now.

22

MASON

Laura hadn't come out of the bedroom when I received a text on my phone. I pulled it out of my pocket and unlocked the screen, frowning at the text that had come from my sister.

She wanted me to come home and it was something urgent.

"Again?"

The question escaped from my mouth. There was always something fucking urgent and it would have to ruin this moment. I wondered if I could be like Laura. Just go and work and get away from all this fucking drama. It was doing my head in. I didn't know what was wrong this time, but I had some idea. I went to the bedroom door and knocked lightly.

"Laura, something's come up at home and I have to head back. Do you think you can come to the hotel, meet me in my room later? Maybe lunch?"

It was as if she was thinking about it. I was about to say

something to her, about the fact she said that she'd at least try, when she blurted out, "Okay. Sounds nice."

I smiled to myself, pulling away from the door.

"I'll see you later," I called out to her. "Hurry up and lock the front door behind me, all right?"

"Okay!"

I hesitated a bit, wanting her to lock it immediately, but stepped out anyway. I dialed my sister's number as I made my way downstairs. She answered just as I stepped out of the building.

"Hey, Emily. What's going—?"

"Don't come home," she said, cutting me off. "Just go to your room back at the hotel, okay? Not back to the mansion."

I frowned, wanting more detail, but she hung up before I could ask for any. I just shrugged and went to my car where I'd parked it a few blocks from Laura's place. I'd walked all the way to the supermarket and carried the stuff I bought for her, plus the food I cooked, all the way to her house, but there wasn't anywhere near her building with a free parking space.

The trek wasn't enough to tire me out. If anything, I nearly skipped the whole way there, but I had my pride and my image to uphold, so I behaved myself.

I made it to my car and jumped in, putting one of my CDs in the player. The drive wasn't that long, but I enjoyed the music for as long as it lasted. I was whistling along as I parked the car at the hotel and jumped out to head inside. I went all the way up to my room, let myself in, and went to take a shower.

Was Emily going to come to my room? I frowned, wondering if she even knew my room number, before shrugging the thought off. It wasn't like she couldn't find out.

Because I hadn't showered yet or brushed my teeth, I stripped down and jumped into the shower. I was done and out, toweling my hair dry in ten minutes. I didn't know how long Emily would take to arrive, so I hurriedly put on some clothes.

By the time I was back in the front room, there was a knock on the door.

"Just in time," I muttered to myself, stepping toward the door to unlock it.

Only the person I expected, was not the person standing there.

"Dad?" I said, incredulous.

"Hello there, Mason," he said casually as if nothing was wrong, but when it came to him everything was wrong.

He was dressed in a suit as per usual, with his hands casually tucked into his pockets. He walked past me into my room, and all I could do was stand and gape at him.

"What the hell are you doing here?" I asked.

"Watch your language," he retorted in warning. "I am your father, you know. And I also happen to own this hotel, so I have every right to be here."

That was enough to break me out of my stupor, and I glared at him. That high handedness right there, I technically had it too, but I'd learned it from him, and it was his one trait that I hated.

"I thought you had a heart attack or were on your death

bed?" I said sarcastically. "It hasn't been nearly long enough for you to make a miraculous recovery, Dad. So what are you doing here? The truth, please. If you're worried I'm going to skip town, you don't have to... yet."

I added that 'yet' just to annoy him. For the moment, I couldn't imagine leaving unless Laura agreed to go with me, and I somehow doubted that she would. Dad turned to look at me with this curious expression on his face but he didn't ask.

"I came to talk about… well, how you're currently living your life."

I sighed and walked over to the couch. It didn't surprise me he had something to criticize. I didn't exactly live the way he'd taught me to. And of course, perfect, slightly controlling Dad that he was, he'd know. There probably hadn't been a scandal about me already because he'd taken care of that end. Rumors inside the hotels where I stayed at never spread out of the hotel because he threw his weight around and made people listen to what he had to say.

Not that I was grateful to him. He'd always been better at doing whatever he wanted and not listening to me at all. My little rebellious phase meant nothing to him, and I'd known, but it doubled as my distraction, so I'd carried on. It would probably come to a stop now.

"Please, Dad," I said, waving a hand to the other chair. "Have a seat and tell me all about your troubles, why don't you."

Again, I was being sarcastic, and I hated the way that he brought that out of me. A few minutes ago, I was on cloud nine. Now I felt as if I was a few steps from torture. I was too old to be feeling like that little boy he could bully all the time. Maybe I should listen to what he has to say, and then tell him exactly what's on my mind.

He chuckled as I moved to sit down, leaning back with his legs crossed and his fingers folded together on his knee.

"I'm here to give you an ultimatum," he said bluntly.

I rolled my eyes, not even surprised. "I guessed it would be something like that. I mean, you couldn't just be a normal dad and ask why I'm going through my angsty teenage years late, and then talk things out with me."

"You are right that isn't my style," he said. "So I'm not going to bother doing any of that. You're an adult now, Mason, not a teenager. And you need to know that all of your actions have consequences."

"Consequences for you, you mean. I don't have a care in the world." I waved a hand around blithely, an indication that I wasn't taking him seriously.

"No, consequences in general," he retorted. "I don't want you to think I'm not grateful for all the work you've done for me up until now, but your behavior is… horrible. And I'm tired of keeping it from your mother. So… you either stop it with the partying, or you're out."

I stared at him, surprised he'd kept it all from Mom. If he'd just told her, she'd have scolded me until I behaved, because I listened to what she wanted. I'd always wondered why she never mentioned it when I went back home.

"Am I banned from all parties in general?" I asked, just to be a smartass. "Like, if a friend asked me to a party, I have to refuse? Even if it's a birthday or a holiday event that could be publicized? Parties the company will be throwing at some of the hotels, where you, Mom, and all of us usually are in attendance?”

“Don’t be difficult, Mason. I’ve let you have your fun over the years, but haven’t you had enough now? All I want is for you to take life seriously from now on because I won’t always be there to cover your ass for you.”

My eyebrow jumped up when he cursed. It wasn’t something he usually did, and he must have been wound up to curse at all.

“Don’t strain yourself, Dad. It’s not a problem, I’ll stop.”

It wasn’t like I particularly cared for the partying, or that any of the people I invited were friends of mine. They were just acquaintances I’d met in my travels. I’d have no trouble cutting ties with most of them.

Besides, even if he hadn't come to see me, I had a feeling I would have stopped anyway, now that I had Laura to think about. Thinking about her led to thinking about what Dad’s reaction would be when I told him I was dating someone, and it might be serious.

He’d been married before, to Trent’s mother. I believed he loved Mom though, because while he was a hardass with the rest of us, the two people in the world that could still make him go soft were Emily and Mom.

There was a problem though. Not only was Laura a maid at his hotel, but she was also several years older than me, and somehow I didn’t think that would go over well with Dad. It had been him who’d drilled into all of us from the time we were young that we were Thompsons, and we had a duty to uphold the family name and image. That we had to act with dignity, in public or not. My taunts to

Emily not to make friends with the help—I got all that from his teachings. And here I was, going above and beyond.

Dad's sure to be fucking proud, I thought with sarcasm.

"I promise to cut it with the wild parties," I said, being sincere. "I'll only go to the parties that you approve of. Now, if that's all you had to say to me, you can let yourself out. I'll get in line so don't worry about it anymore."

Matthew Thompson didn't take orders from anyone, but he had nothing more to say to me, so he just got up and left. A part of me was disappointed he didn't even try to talk to me, though it was completely expected. I was a little worried about when he'd find out about Laura, but not enough to stop him.

When the time came, I'd just have to make Dad listen to me. For the moment, I couldn't be bothered. I was waiting for Laura to come to me, and I couldn't let her see me all gloomy or she'd get worried unnecessarily.

Hopefully, Dad's conviction to have a woman he loved would be extended to his children and their choices. He could butt in with everything else, but I hoped that in this one matter, he'd fucking trust me.

For the moment, Laura won't try running from me again. I had to convince her we could have something real together, so in case I had to go up against my dad, she wouldn't leave me.

I didn't think she would, but… you never knew.

23

LAURA

I waited until Mason left and then hesitated as I peeked my head out the door, to make sure he'd left. I took a deep breath knowing he'd gone and went to lock the door. Then I turned around and dramatically fell back against it.

What exactly was I going to do about Mason Thompson? I'd had such conviction when I told myself that, no matter how disappointed or how tempted I was, I wouldn't waver. And yet, I'd gone way beyond that. We were dating now! I'd given him permission to be my boyfriend, so why was I so scared? Why did I have butterflies in my stomach at the thought of it?

For one reason only, Mason had never dated. He was still young but this was Mason Thompson, the guy who, whenever pictured at official events and various parties, always had a woman on his arm. And of all people, he decided to ask me.

"I can't believe it," I murmured to myself, but I was grinning and no longer scared but happy about being that girl. The one he wanted to date, compared to all the rest who were most likely prettier, sexier or richer than me. None of them made him change his mind, only me.

The fact he'd never actually dated and wanted me to be his girlfriend… I had to admit, it was pretty sweet. So even though I was berating myself for giving into him once again, I didn't regret it. If anything, I just wanted to see him more!

"But first, a proper shower."

Before, I'd only jumped under the shower spray for a minute to clean up from last night. I'd been too impatient to see him and I could hear him cooking in my kitchen, so I'd toweled down, then dressed in some old clothes I found lying around and tried to act calm when I went out to see him. He must have bought the act, which was good because I didn't need him to see just how much he affected me, or he'd use it against me in the future, I just knew it.

As I went to the bathroom, I turned on the stereo and played some music from the radio. I left the music loud so I could hear it over my shower, though my neighbors would probably complain of noise again if it went on for too long. I hummed along as I listened to the music, my secret weakness: punk from the early 2000s.

The song switched to one of my favorite bands to date, Green Day. I'd listened to the song enough times to have it all memorized, and I sang along loud and horribly off key.

Back in college, my study had been in music. I'd figured

back then that if I loved it enough to want to listen to it all the time, I should try my hand at making my own. My reasons for picking the major may have been simple, but I'd thrown myself into it. I'd wanted to sing, but even back then, I knew I probably didn't have a chance at it. I might have gotten a voice coach, gone through several practices and caught a glimmer of hope. But no matter how much I liked it, it was the easiest thing in the world to give up when the time came.

The playlist moved on, and another song I'd heard over and over but couldn't get tired of went on. I hummed quietly to listen properly to the lyrics, because it always hit me right in the feels, and especially so at that moment. The song told a tale of first love and how it was lost. Saying 'fuck it all' to love, because it could be painful whether you had it or you didn't.

Considering my current situation with Mason, I thought the song was very apt. It made me wonder what would become of us, if I would end up like the subject of the song, alone and singing in my shower to old music like one of those women who refused to stop using two cans of hairspray a day to keep their 1980s hairstyle from falling.

In the fantasy, my hair was long and straight, I didn't have a specific hairstyle, nor would I ever, but the dream was so vivid I shuddered just thinking about it.

Before Mason, I'd only ever had the one real boyfriend. He was the guy who stuck it out with me for nearly a year. In college, I'd mostly just done a few one-night stands, and my first attempt at dating failed miserably in a couple of weeks, so I couldn't even count it. I didn't even mind, because I was serious about college, no matter how slim my chances were of getting the ending I wanted. I hadn't known then that I had to cherish the time I had while I was healthy. I'd wasted it.

Then I got sick.

After the cancer treatments, the first two guys I tried to date couldn't stick around for long after they'd seen me naked because it bothered them. It was around that time I decided to have a nipple tattoo to replace the one cut out after the surgery, covering up the scars that remained behind.

I may have been judging Mason too harshly, because considering my previous experience, he was by far the best. Besides him being younger, and annoying me in the beginning, there was nothing wrong with him. It was a little strange thinking of him that way, but the thought certainly rang true, and it made me feel a little better about my decision like it wasn't entirely the wrong choice.

The water cooled down, and I yelped and turned it off, coming back to myself. I didn't know how long I'd drifted off, but I needed to get out before my skin started to shrivel up.

Even once I had the shower off, I still didn't move. Instead, I stared at the shower walls as thoughts ran through my mind.

"I'm dating Mason Thompson," I said out loud and shivered.

Darn, it didn't even feel real. The Thompson name was

such a big name to everyone that worked at the hotel. Heck, it was even a part of the hotel's name! Even when a guest wasn't necessarily related to the Thompson family, if they had the same name, the staff made sure to look out for them specifically. It was made into a rule.

Everyone would flip if they ever found out the news, not that I was going to tell them. I wasn't even sure when I would tell Jessi. I had to tell her with her being my best friend and all. I'd have to muster up some courage to manage it, but I could get through it later.

A draft went through my bathroom, and I shivered because I was just standing there, all wet, and I got out and picked up a towel to wipe myself down. Then I picked an outfit, one of my best, and slowly pulled it on.

Was this... going to be okay? Even if we were just trying, I was already in too deep with this kid, falling even deeper would probably just bring worse results later on. At the moment, I could at least put up with my disappointment. Eventually, I'd move on. But if we got closer, it would be harder.

Sure, for the moment, Mason rocked my world. I couldn't keep lying to myself and claim he meant nothing at all when that was not the case. But that didn't mean any of the problems I'd thought of before were suddenly gone. If anything, now that we were trying and it wasn't just a one-night thing, I'd probably get to see it all clearly when I wasn't sure I wanted to.

Could I take this chance? Or, the more appropriate question, *should* I take this chance? Because after that time I'd been sick, I'd decided to make sure I lived without regrets, and this didn't feel like one of those times where regrets wouldn't crop up. I was happy, sure, but I also couldn't help but be uneasy about everything, and didn't that speak volumes? If I couldn't just be wholly happy with this…

"What are you talking about, you stubborn girl?" I scolded myself, interrupting the negative thoughts.

After everything, what was my motto now? In spite of all my regrets, I would always look forward to the bright side. So why was I sabotaging myself by thinking about all the things that could go bad?

If regret happened down the line, then I could deal with it then. I had to admit, if only to myself, that if I let this chance pass me by and ignored it instead of trying to work toward it, I would regret not trying at all when it was something I was already losing sleep over.

"He said he trusted me," I muttered, picking up my mirror and looking at my frowny face. "He said he trusts me, so…"

As fake as his pretty words had sounded, I completely believed everything he said because it was probably the sincerest I'd ever seen him. He didn't look like the kind of man who divulged his secrets to people easily, so it would only be fair if I responded in kind, right?

I was going to try and trust in him. The moment he broke it, I'd probably run, but for the moment I had no reason to.

"Please Mason," I said with a sigh. "Don't give me a reason not to trust you, okay?"

I finished getting myself dressed, and realized I still had

some time. So I finally sat down to continue the knitting from last night with the little time I had to wait before lunch. I kept checking the time as I worked, not sure exactly when he wanted me to arrive anyway, growing ever so impatient as the time ticked away slowly.

24

LAURA

My nerves started to get the better of me as I threw the knitting aside. It was mostly done. All that was left was the bottom of the hat, then I could add it to the new pile. Usually, I would use my day off to knit and watch some TV because I only ever got the one day off a week.

It was half an hour past noon, but I figured it was enough time. I got up and packed my things away. I hesitated a little in my room, not sure if I was supposed to take anything with me. In the end, I picked one of my small purses and put in some money, my cards, and my phone. Then I left the apartment.

I took the walk plenty of times, usually every day when going to work unless it got too cold out, but today the distance felt especially great. I practically jogged most of the way there and stopped a way off from the hotel to catch my breath. I looked down at myself, feeling a bit self-conscious. This was probably the dressiest I'd ever looked near the hotel, in a pencil skirt that tied at the waist and went down just a bit above the knees, and a white blouse with a black polka dot collar, with frills down the front.

What if someone I worked with saw me?

It probably won't happen, I tried to psych myself up. Most of them have time off too, or they'd be working. So there was no reason why they should see me, right?

I couldn't steer clear of *all* the staff.

"Jessi lives here," I said aloud to myself, a little surprised I'd forgotten this fact. Jessi had been given a small room at the hotel that she'd stayed at. It wasn't a consideration that was given to just anyone, and it cut quite a bit out of her salary every month to stay there, but her place was at least better looking than mine.

If anyone asked, I could just say I was visiting my friend. She'd back me up.

With a deep breath, I walked into the hotel. I kept my head down, fingers holding tight to the straps of my purse. I was so tense, feeling like I might be stopped on the way, but no one stopped me when I got to the elevator. It was one of the few times that I wasn't using the staff elevators, and even as I breathed a sigh of relief when the doors closed, leaving me alone, I couldn't help but still be anxious.

When the doors opened on the right floor, I practically ran to Mason's door, then hesitated some more before knocking on it. He only took a moment to answer the door though, grinning when he saw it was me there.

"Hey. I almost thought you wouldn't make it."

I frowned. "I'm not that late, am I?"

"Nah. I just had a visitor I wasn't expecting, so I got a little impatient waiting for you to get here."

I froze, then peeked around him. "Visitor…?"

"Don't worry, he's gone and he won't be coming back. Give me a minute, and we'll head out."

He left the door open as he walked further into the room, and I took it to mean I could wait inside. I stayed right by the door after I closed it behind me. He only took a minute, coming back while pulling on his coat.

"Where exactly are we going?" I asked as he let us out of the room. "I thought you were going to make me something?"

I was a little anxious walking around the hotel with Mason, in case anyone else saw. His big frame stuck pretty close to my side, so I hoped most people would just be looking at him and ignore that I was right there. He had that kind of presence.

"I didn't say I was going to cook you anything. At this point, it would be fairer if you cooked me a meal first." He arched an eyebrow at me, and I felt my face flush.

Right. I'd forgotten that he'd cooked for me three times already. I just didn't think anything I could make could be up to his standards.

"So, what are we doing now?"

"Right now, I'm taking you out to eat. It'll be a surprise where. I thought we could both benefit from a day spent outside."

I didn't say any more and followed after him. We made our way outside the hotel, stopping at his car. He opened the door for me, then walked around to his seat. He put on some music for the ride, and I hummed along to the songs I knew as we spent the time mostly silent. I was curious about where exactly it was we were going.

By the time we got there, passing a post that let me know I wasn't wrong in my thinking, I was gaping.

"Mooresville? To a restaurant on Lake Norman?"

The lake was a huge one, and manmade from what I knew, created by Duke Power to supply energy to North Carolina. It was still used for the same reason, but the artificial waterline had created a boom in lake-front properties and shops catering to an upmarket crowd. The lake was also used for water sports like sailing, and even had a few showboats for dinner and entertainment on the water.

I'd heard of it ever since I got to North Carolina, and I'd always been curious about it, but never enough to make my way there. Especially since the shores were now polluted with lake houses that were pretty much McMansions for the rich. I'd heard there was a public shore where people could go and admire the sights, but I'd never had enough courage to go there.

Mason, of course, didn't take us to the public area. He took a turn somewhere, and I noticed how much closer we were getting to those expensive looking houses.

"Your house isn't out here, is it?" I asked.

"Of course not," he retorted. "Dad wanted the family mansion to be further inland, so it is. We do have a small house out here though," he admitted.

I shot him an incredulous look because there weren't any houses in the vicinity that I would exactly call 'small.'

"Is that where we're going?"

"Nah. The family only visits there occasionally, but Dad would still know if any of us stayed over there on our own. We won't be going anywhere near the house."

As he spoke, he took another road that led us closer to the lake.

"Isn't it a little strange? I mean, your house is less than forty-five minutes from this lake, so why on earth would you still have another one in the same area?"

He shrugged. "You'd have to ask my Dad to answer that question, I never really bothered to ask him."

"As if that would ever happen," I said with a snort.

The car eventually came to a stop and Mason got out. I scrambled to follow after him, and he led us even closer to the lake. I wondered if we were going to have a shore side picnic or something, but then we reached the docks, and I was gaping again when I saw where we were going.

"Is that a yacht?"

"Yeah," Mason said, glancing at me over the shoulder. "It's the family's sailing yacht. I mean, technically it's Dad's, but anyone can use it whenever it's free because he's rarely ever on it. I have lunch waiting for us onboard."

My steps slowed, but I still followed after him as he made his way to the expensive looking boat. Was this the reason they had another house by the lake? Was it necessary, just for them to dock their yacht there? I didn't think so…

"What are you doing?" Mason called, making me jump. "You're lagging behind, Laura. Come on."

I was feeling a little overwhelmed, being close to something that probably cost more than I could ever earn in my lifetime. Then again, just about everything surrounding Mason made me think that way. Still, seeing him standing there, holding his hand out to me, it lessened the need to run just a little. I picked up speed, then slid my hand into his, and we walked together to the yacht.

Getting on it was an adventure on its own. Mason had to help me, and I was scared of falling the entire time. I couldn't swim, so large bodies of water tended to scare me.

"I hope you don't get seasick," Mason said.

"I... don't know," I answered truthfully.

"Then we'll just have to find out."

With that, he set us out, starting the yacht's engine and steering us a little further into the lake, but not too far. The shore at least looked close enough to swim to, even if it looked like it would be a long swim. There were plenty of life vests on the boat too, so I could breathe. The swaying of the boat was disorienting at first, but I quickly grew used to it. I'd probably feel a little queasy by the time we got back.

Mason expertly handled the boat, letting the sails do the work after a while, and steered us into a quiet cove, where I could see the orange of the dirt on the shore. He set the anchor and turned back to me with a smile.

"Come over here," Mason called out to me once more.

He was giving me his hand, and again, I took it. He led us around the outside of the cabin, to the back of the boat. I gasped when I saw a table fully set like something from a restaurant—with an expensive tablecloth, silverware, and food—covered by an umbrella so there'd be some shade.

"I didn't make it this time, but I hope you still like the

food," Mason was saying, as he led me forward then pulled a chair out for me. "I hope I got everything we need here, but if there's something you want, you can ask me. There's some wine, and some snacks below and I thought we could hang out here for the rest of the day. Just us, where nobody could get to us."

So, we ate, soaked in some sun, and lazed around on the deck. Later, we had some of the wine and cheese snacks, and it was all very pleasant and sweet.

As great as it all was, I couldn't help feeling a little down, wondering if he'd change. And after going through such a luxurious afternoon, by the time we were on our way back, I wondered if I even wanted him to change, and that was probably a dangerous thought to have.

25

MASON

The last few weeks had been fucking amazing. If I'd known that being with a woman like Laura could feel like this, then I would have done it a long time ago. Yet no one had sparked that kind of interest in me until now. No one but Laura. She really was special even if she didn't feel it at the best of times. She was the kind of woman who made me feel so small. She seemed to think that because I was rich that I was in some crazy way superior to her. But she beat cancer and came up on top with a smile on her face all the time.

It was as if nothing could get her down and I had no intention of making her sad. I felt that I had something else to work towards and aspire to and that was being a good boyfriend. It was so much better than trying to be the perfect son. I knew I'd finally grown up in a short space of time and things could only get better.

I knew Laura had to work but she didn't avoid me. She stopped by my room earlier, just as I was about to leave, and I cut five minutes out of her time for a long make-out session before we both had to get to work.

Days went by, and things only got better, even more amazing. I'd take Laura home in the evenings, and at times she'd invite me in. Or I'd have her come to my hotel room after work hours, and she'd spend the time with me. Sex happened, but it was so much more than that. We talked, and it was a nice surprise to learn we had some things in common. She was shocked when I told her about my past rugby career, though she'd teased me for being the typical high school jock.

I was fucking kidding myself if I thought that I just liked her. It was more than that. I was falling in love, hook, line, and sinker. I was fairly confident I wasn't the only one, as Laura got less and less shy about us being together, and smiled every time she saw me, before worrying about what others would see or think.

We weren't secretive, and I didn't care if the whole world knew about us. More to the point, I *wanted* everyone to know about us. I was so proud to go out with her and have her on my arm and let everyone know she was my girl. No one else's, just mine.

Things with Dad got a little easier too, even though it was technically still me following his orders and ultimatums. Still, it was probably the one time I was happy to follow his orders, and he wasn't avoiding talking to me anymore. He sought me out more often than I wanted actually because most of my attention was centered around Laura now, but we'd more or less made up.

I hadn't told him about Laura yet, but I had a feeling

he'd guessed something must have changed with me. Even Trent remarked once that I looked happier, which meant he must have seen through me before because the only difference was that my satisfied and still somewhat care-free attitude was genuine.

Within that time, I cleaned up my act, or at least I tried. I hadn't had a party in a while because I was so busy, and I didn't feel like having any anyway. The people on my friends list kept calling me up, and I'd give some excuse or outright ignore their calls, knowing that eventually, they'd stop trying to contact me and find some other idiot willing to foot their bill.

With everything else outside of my work, it still felt like I failed sometimes. Particularly with Laura.

We weren't just sneaking around to each other's places. She was the first person I'd ever dated, and I was insistent on taking her out. She didn't seem to mind, but some-times… it wasn't that she looked at me with disappoint-ment or anything, but with my latent talent of reading people, I could tell when she wasn't exactly happy, even though she went along with whatever I wanted.

On her days off, I took her to other parts of North Carolina to explore and spend some time outside. It had been a surprise to me to learn she hadn't explored much of the state after moving, though the fact she'd moved late to the state didn't surprise me at all, with her slight accent. But then there was this way she stared at the hiking trails we passed on our way to our destinations, that told me she'd rather do that than go wherever I was taking her.

Then when I'd propose we eat out, she'd recommend

cheap food places. Also, she hadn't cooked for me. Every time I brought it up, she'd keep saying next time, and I let it go. And even after all those days passed and we grew closer, she still didn't like to accept presents from me.

I didn't understand why.

Before, I'd taken the initiative, and it was the wrong one. My intentions at the time weren't above reproach, I'd pretty much seen her as she'd accused me—as a trinket—but I'd changed my thinking, hadn't I? So why did she still insist on fighting me when all I was trying to do was take care of her?

It left me puzzled, and there was nowhere I could go to look for answers. I was a little afraid of talking to her about it because while she'd said she wouldn't run, I feared to give her reasons to want to. I would rather try to rectify the mistake on my own and go to her only after it had failed. But I had to try at least!

The next time Trent let me have the day off, I went back to the mansion, texting my sister to meet me in the lounge on the first floor closest to the foyer. She could be anywhere around the house or the grounds, and if I didn't contact her beforehand, finding her would be a pain.

By the time I arrived, she was there waiting for me, with a tea set on the coffee table, with two cups and two side plates of assorted pastries and cookies. I arched my eyebrows at it and couldn't help but take a dig at her.

"Is it tea time already? No dolls this time, Emily?" I teased, reminding her of all those times as a kid when she wanted to have a 'tea party,' and she'd get Mom to make me and Kevin join her because she didn't have that many friends in her private school.

She looked at me with a frown. "No, Mason, my dolls will not be joining us today. They abhor your manners."

I rolled my eyes and took a seat across from her. I poured myself some of the tea, picked up a pastry and sat back to eat. It was past lunch already and I'd eaten, but I didn't mind a little snack.

"Now," Emily said, pouring herself some tea. "Why don't you tell me what this trip is about, big brother? You wouldn't just come here to see me."

"Why not?" I retorted, feeling crap that she'd spoiled my good mood.

She arched an eyebrow. "Don't forget I know you. If this were just another visit, you'd have arrived then looked for me, not called me out to wait for you."

I hummed, slowly nodding my head like I understood what she said. My attention had already wavered, as I thought of how to bring up my current issues.

"I did have a question for you," I said after long minutes of silence. I would have held out longer, but I was feeling impatient, and she noticed, perking up.

"Oh? What could you possibly want to know from me? It couldn't be woman trouble, right? The ladies love you."

I sighed, and her eyes widened as she concluded rightfully that this was the problem.

"So, there's this woman I'm seeing, and she's not like any of the women I've been with before, so get that out of your head. You could say… she's a woman that's used to being around ordinary people. Well, people not raised in our world."

"Ah," she said, nodding in understanding. "It's not someone at the mansion, right? Maybe at the hotel?"

I hesitated a little on whether or not I should give this detail, but in the end, I decided there was nothing particularly wrong with it.

"At the hotel. Her name… is Laura."

I didn't get the time to add more because Emily spurted out the sip of tea she was taking. I could only watch with my mouth open. She set the cup down with a loud clink and leveled a glare at me.

"Tell me you did not just say 'Laura'? Are there two of them working at the hotel, or what? Because you better not mean who I'm thinking of."

I arched an eyebrow, taken aback by the passionate response. Did she somehow know Laura? It was a surprise, only because Laura worked at the hotel, and Emily rarely ever went there. Laura had never been to the mansion, so how could the two have ever met?

"It could be the same person," I said slowly. "Because as far as I know, there's only one Laura working at the hotel…"

"Are you playing with her?" she immediately demanded. "She's my friend too, Mason, so you better not be using her for one of your games. I mean, I don't speak to her as often as I speak to Jessi, but you definitely will get into trouble with me if I hear from either of them that you made her cry."

I frowned. "Who the hell is Jessi, anyway? And why the

hell do you think I'd make her cry? I just told you I'm dating her, have I ever said that to you about a woman before?"

That was enough to give her pause, and she relaxed a little, though she was still frowning.

"You're dating. Huh," she repeated to herself. "What exactly have you done together?"

I arched an eyebrow but guessed she didn't mean in the bedroom. My little sister might be twenty-one but she was still way too young to know about that side of relationships. At least in my opinion. As far as I knew, she'd never had a crush on someone in real life, maybe some of the boy bands and actors she watched on TV. So I told her everything I'd done with Laura so far. There was plenty more I wanted the two of us to experience together, but I didn't mention those just yet because it was a pretty long list.

"You're doing it all wrong," she declared, once I was finished.

"What do you mean, all wrong?" I asked, narrowing my eyes.

"This is why, big brother, I always say you're smart but a little stupid. Just think about it. At least you stopped it with the gifts but what you're doing right now isn't any better. As far as I know, Laura's always led a pretty simple, but sometimes hard life. It's never gonna be about your money or the gifts with her. If you want your relationship with her to go well, then what you bring into it, besides the riches, will matter more. Try doing things for her, simple things, instead of throwing the world at her feet, because it's only going to make her uncomfortable."

I understood what Emily was saying. I knew this much, like when I made her dinner and bought her groceries instead of taking expensive candy and flowers to her apartment that night. I still did that, and she was happy every time, but…

"I want to do more for her," I admitted. "She's the first woman I've cared this much about, Emily. I want to do… everything I've ever wanted to do with her. But that's wrong?"

She sighed, rolling her eyes at me like I was the biggest idiot in the universe. A look that hadn't changed much since she was five and trying to get me to do things for her.

"That's fine and all, but why don't you start slow? Like, you know, doing what she wants to do first, then moving on to what you want to do later, but explain it to her. You could take her to her favorite places, for example, not just where you want to go. It would go over better, at least in the beginning. Because basically, what you've been doing is showing her that she's missing something from life. From our perspective maybe it is but to her, it's like telling her that her life wasn't good enough, that she should be aiming higher. She might not want to do that."

I sighed and leaned back in my seat, running a hand down my face. Emily was right; I'd been acting the idiot about this whole thing, like taking one step forward and two steps back.

"If you want to treat her right," Emily continued, "then talk to her about things, don't just assume. Laura would want the simple things, like going to diners and Mexican restaurants instead of luxury lunch in the family yacht or taking her somewhere expensive. She'll want to go to the library, or to the hiking trails. It's all she needs; you just have to focus on it."

I nodded slowly. I would never have thought I'd be listening to my little sister talk to me about how to do right by a woman, but that was where I found myself. I had to compromise what I wanted to do if it would make Laura comfortable, make her happy.

So Emily spent the afternoon, and well most of the evening, giving me a long talk about the difference in life-style between me and a woman like Laura.

26

MASON

After Emily set me straight, I left the mansion to go back to the hotel. I wanted to find Laura so we could talk right then and there. I didn't know how much damage I'd done with my behavior, and I felt like I needed to fix it as quickly as possible.

But when I got to my room and picked up the phone to call for the cleaning department, I paused, knowing this would only make her even more annoyed with me. So I put the hotel phone back down, then wandered around my apartment.

"Why am I still living in a fucking hotel room?" I muttered to myself.

Initially, I'd moved into the hotel instead of the mansion for a couple of reasons. One, it would be more convenient to be closer to work. The second, and the biggest, reason was that I didn't think I could behave, and I didn't want to expose my mom and my sister to that side of my life. Not to mention I didn't want to be too close to Dad's scrutiny.

It was always meant to be temporary though. After all, even though I had to move around for the sake of my work, I still had someplace to go home to. Not the mansion, no. I visited, but I'd stopped thinking of it as home a while back. I couldn't live with my parents forever, no matter how big their place was.

I'd bought my little space ages ago, where I lived on my own and no one, not even a member of my family, had ever stepped a foot in it. It was out of the state though.

Maybe I needed some place closer?

With that thought in mind, I went to take my laptop out of my things in the bedroom. The hotel had Wi-Fi set up for all the rooms, and I moved with the laptop to the couch, turning it on.

I made a quick search of possible houses for sale. I narrowed down a few locations in my price range. I ignored the pricier, larger places. I had funds in my own account that I'd use to pay for the house, and while I could afford something bigger, it was the last thing I wanted.

Then, I found it. I was just browsing around on this realtor's website when I saw the picture, and it made me freeze. I clicked on it and fell in love instantly. I checked the information and decided I wanted to see it in real life. I was done with work for the day, so there wouldn't be anything to hold me back. Just in case, I sent a message to Laura to tell her I wouldn't be taking her home later. I didn't do it every day, and she insisted it was safe enough that I'd stopped nagging her about it.

On my way out, I made a call.

"Hello? I'm calling to get some more information about a house…"

I was done speaking by the time I got into my car to head out. I'd transferred the information from the website to my phone already, and I input the address in my car's GPS, though I already knew the general direction I was supposed to head toward.

The drive wasn't too long, just under an hour at average speed. If I went faster, skirting the speed limit, it could be faster. As I got near, I looked at the surroundings and decided it was just as perfect. There wouldn't be any neighbors too close…

The house was on the outskirts of Charlotte, away from the bustle and much closer to the foothills, in the area where the flatlands met the mountains and it got a bit hilly. I'd already got permission to look through it without someone present because I'd only be checking out the outside. If I didn't like it inside, it could be remodeled.

"Perfect," I murmured.

It was simple. A one-story house, clapboard and painted white with blue shutters. The house was private, it even had a picket fence, and there was a tire swinging in a tree in the front yard. There was an area for a garden, a garage to the side of the house. Pretty much everything one would need for a simple life.

"I'd need to check out the backyard," I said to myself. "Add some improvements, check the inside and see if I need to remodel anything…"

Different plans whirled around in my head. This was

different from the last time. Before, I'd had a professional realtor take me around, and I picked a place with just enough space for me and was private enough while staying secure. I'd paid for it, and that was that.

This time, it wouldn't just be me staying here because I knew it was just the perfect place to build the life I wanted, one with Laura in it. The house looked big enough from the outside to house more than two people. There might be children in the future, there might not. I didn't know if I even wanted to be a father, if Laura could even have kids. Or maybe we could adopt if Laura wanted to, a kid that already had potty training, if we were going to go that route.

All of this, though, was exactly what I'd been missing in my life. I had an okay family. I loved my mom and sister especially, and I was closer to Kevin and still somewhat distant with Dad and Trent. The fact that neither I nor my brothers wanted to live too close to home spoke volumes, and I'd always thought when I was growing up, if we didn't have so many riches, I could have been happier. As long as we were comfortable. To have an understanding father instead of a demanding one would have been nice too.

We were a family, but not as close as other families I'd seen, and not just on TV. Normal families where everybody sat together to eat, not because it was mandatory, but because it was tradition, and they wanted to. This normalcy, with a loving home, and a woman that loved me…

I could practically picture it, and it was beautiful.

Once I felt satisfied with what I'd seen, I got back in my car to drive back to the hotel.

I wanted to marry her.

I'd had the thought for a while now, but it had never been quite so strong before. I was a decisive kind of guy though, and I didn't hesitate with what I wanted, so if I was going to buy a house for the two of us to move into, I wanted us to be married or at least engaged when I asked her to move in with me.

How would I break this news to her? I had no idea. It would take some serious planning because I wanted the proposal to go off without a hitch. Maybe have a key at the ready, instead of a ring, or both, when I asked? I thought up and dismissed, considered, and readjusted several ideas.

More than anything, I wanted to be what Laura deserved. I wanted her to be happy when she was with me because she'd made me the happiest I'd been in years.

27

LAURA

The way things were going with Mason, I'd never be alone again. I wanted to be with him all the time. I felt as if I was on drugs, the same ones I took when I was on chemotherapy and without them I couldn't function at times, even though they did make me feel sick. But with Mason, it wasn't like that. It was a good feeling. I felt on top of the world when I was with him. He'd go out of his way to make me feel special all the time.

I was slowly but surely understanding what it meant to be in love. I'd been alone for far too long, the idea of sharing my life with another person had never come into the picture. Now, I couldn't imagine being without him and the crazy part was I was getting the impression that he felt exactly the same way. Before, us being together seemed so wrong, but now it felt so natural.

After work, I changed into casual clothes and sat in the staff lounge waiting for Jessi. I had the chance to do something new, or I could have gone home and knitted, but I didn't feel like it. It had been a while since Jessi and I had hung out.

"Laura! Were you waiting for me? You didn't have to."

I looked up to see Jessi just coming out of the kitchens. I smiled brightly at her, then waved enthusiastically, though considering how few people there were in the room, she'd have noticed me anyway. She just smiled at my antics.

"Just let me get changed first, all right?"

"Okay!"

I sat back and waited for her, watching as the other employees hurried and left for their homes. It reminded me of my curiosity before, about the living arrangements. I was pretty sure Jessi was the only one with that kind of luxury.

She was back minutes later, and I grabbed my things so we could leave together.

"Hey," she said, arms open and leaning forward for a hug I received gladly. "What's up? You're looking happy."

I bit my lip at the smile that wanted to come out.

"Forget about that. I wanted to ask if I could come up to your room tonight. It's been so long since we've just talked, I wanted to catch up."

She shrugged. "Of course, I could never say no to you."

I followed her as she went to the staff elevator, and we both got in. I hung back as she pressed the button for her floor, and we rose up.

"Your floor is pretty high up," I commented. "How did I not notice that before?"

"You probably just didn't pay attention before," she suggested.

I hummed without answering, but I knew that wasn't it. It was because of Mason. Since I'd been going up to his room to meet him, it occurred to me how close Jessi's floor was to his. I just never took stock before, because it didn't matter to me before what floor her apartment was on.

We got out of the elevator and she led the way. She let us in with her keycard, and I slid off my shoes as I walked over to the couch and sat on it with my legs tucked under me, holding one of the pillows to my chest.

"Would you like to have something to eat now?" Jessi asked as she continued to the kitchenette. "I could whip something up for us right now if you'd like."

"I'm fine for now," I said hurriedly. "I just really wanted to catch up, it's been a while and it feels as if we're almost strangers these days rather than best friends."

I didn't mean to make her feel guilty, the fault wasn't really hers, it was more mine.

"Okay," she said, stopping. "That sounds good."

She took off her coat and draped it over the back of the single seat, then joined me on the couch, sitting on the other end of it and eyeing me curiously.

"If we're catching up, why don't you tell me what has you so happy lately? Every time I see you now you're always smiling, and you look more relaxed than I've ever seen you."

That was probably because I felt the most relaxed I had in a while. I tried to erase the guilty expression on my face, but I wasn't good at hiding my feelings. A trait I'd picked up from my Mom and could never erase. She used to tell me all the time it was in the genes and it must be, because I could never hide when I was happy and certainly not when I was down. I knew it was all because of Mason and the new relationship we had. I'd been doubtful in the beginning, but he was a thoughtful boyfriend, and every time he showed that side of himself I was on cloud nine.

There was a downside to all of it though. Because I knew I couldn't continue to be so happy, and I was scared.

"I'd… rather talk about something else, actually," I admitted. "Something… that's a secret."

She tilted her head a little, and I could tell I'd piqued her interest. I never really let on that I had secrets, whether or not she knew that I had them. I would have liked for us to talk about happier things first, but I knew better than to hold this off.

"What is it?" she asked with some trace of concern after I stayed quiet for too long.

"It's something I've wanted to tell you for a while, and I didn't know how to exactly." I bit my lip as my heart started beating faster. There was more on my mind than just Mason and our relationship, there was something I hadn't even told him yet. I knew I would have too, and soon, but I'd put it off. I had to get it out to someone though, and right now, I wanted that person to be my best friend. "You see, before… when I was in college. I got ill… Jessi, I was diagnosed with breast cancer."

Her eyes widened, and she looked like I'd just punched her right in the chest.

"What?" she choked out.

"That's not the most important part," I continued. "I went through surgery and treatments, and it was fine. But the thing is, Jess… when you're a cancer survivor, it's recommended that you keep going for hospital visits to have yourself checked out, in case the cancer comes back."

She just kept blinking at me, looking so confused, and I hated that I was springing this on her out of the blue.

"So you went for a checkup recently?"

I nodded slowly. I'd done it one of the days Mason was busy. He didn't know about my regular hospital visits because I'd been afraid of how he'd react. I couldn't muster up the courage to tell him, but I was feeling scared, and I had a friend I felt I could confide in, unlike the last time. It was too scary to go through that sort of pain alone, darn it!

"I went for a check-up this week… my results didn't come out clean as I've come to expect over the past few years." I could feel my expression crumple, and I didn't stop it. "There's a new lump," I explained. "It's under my other arm, not the side I had to have operated on. They want me to go back soon for more tests."

"Oh, Laura," she whispered, leaning forward and pulling me into another hug as tears started dripping from my eyes.

I held onto her for a moment, because I needed her strength, feeling like I had none of my own at the moment. She rubbed soothing circles on my back, and I sniffled as I tried to hold back even more crying.

"How can I help you?" Jessi asked because she was a great friend like that.

"I don't want to go back to the hospital alone," I admitted. "The last time, I couldn't stand to tell my friends. We were all in college, and I didn't think it would be fair to burden any of them. But I don't think I can do this on my own this time. I'm terrified. Please would you go to the hospital with me?"

"Of course," she said immediately. "When?"

"Tomorrow."

As I spat the word out, I felt guilty already for sharing this with her and not Mason. He should be the one I should be wanting to take me to the hospital and that I should be sharing my news with, but I didn't want to. I couldn't be completely dependent on him all the time. We had to have some space some of the time. It would be too unhealthy otherwise, and besides, he'd think of me as a burden. He treated me like a princess and I wanted him to keep thinking of me as one. Not this older woman that could possibly be sick. I couldn't bear the look on his face if it was bad news.

"All right. I'll take the day off for tomorrow. I'm sure they can deal without me for one day in the kitchen. You'll stay tonight, and we'll go whenever you want. For now, let me get us both something to eat."

I didn't stop her as she went this time because I was feeling hungry. I hadn't been able to eat properly since I got the news, and now that I'd told someone, half that burden was suddenly gone. I could have just told Mason… but I didn't think I was going to.

I lay back on the couch as Jessi cooked. Usually, we would do this sort of thing together, but now that I was seated down, I felt like I'd fall if I tried to get up. I'd been feeling a bit drained lately, getting tired quicker while I worked. Mason was still picking me up from my apartment on some mornings, and he'd been there today. The biggest reason I'd wanted to come up to Jessi's place was that I wasn't positive I could make it all the way home on foot, and Mason was busy. I could have taken a taxi, but then there were all those stairs in my building. It had been a nightmare just getting myself down this morning when my legs felt as if they could go out from under me at any moment.

There were other feelings, other sensations that felt familiar from before. When I started feeling it, I hadn't thought much about it, putting it all down to all the sex I'd been having, and the work. But that doctor's visit had told me everything I needed to know.

I'd left that place with my body trembling. I didn't want to be ill again. As much as I'd tried to be happy after surviving it the first time if it was cancer again, I knew I'd fall apart. Why did it have to be right now, of all times, when I was so genuinely happy? There was no way I could be as brave, or as strong to just go through this alone a second time.

Which was why I was so glad to have Jessi. It was just like her, to agree to take me on the spot, and to take the day off to do it. I did feel a bit guilty for imposing on her, but even more than that, I was grateful.

As I sat there waiting for her to come back with dinner, I could feel the tears fall down my face faster instead of slowing down. It felt like my heart was breaking, even though I had a best friend willing to do a lot for me and a boyfriend who genuinely cared for me. I should have been at my happiest, and yet...

I didn't want to face the treatments. I knew I would have to because I knew there was no choice if I wanted to get better.

My phone vibrated in my pocket, and it was so unexpected that I jumped and let out a gasp.

"What is it?" Jessi asked, ever alert.

I glanced at her in her kitchenette, cutting up veggies for our meal.

"It's nothing. A call just surprised me."

I pulled the phone out of my pocket, only to suck in a sharp breath when I saw Mason's name on the screen. I didn't even hesitate to swipe the call, rejecting it. Then I switched off my phone.

There was no way I could talk to him in the state I was in. I was just barely holding back from breaking down in sobs. There was a chance the lump could be nothing. It might be as simple as going under the knife again to have it cut out to get rid of the problem. But, until I knew for sure, I wasn't going to be able to face him or tell him.

28

LAURA

Jessi set the alarm pretty early, and it woke both of us up. We were close, and we didn't feel particularly embarrassed, so we'd spent last night in the same bed, Jessi holding me as I fell asleep, and that was how we woke.

"I'll go shower first," she said quietly, slipping out of bed.

I watched her leave before I got up. I'd have to borrow some clothes from her for the day because I didn't feel like taking a pit stop at my apartment. She was slightly plump from all the sweet things she ate, but then I couldn't blame her for having a sweet tooth. She made a lot of desserts and pastries for events. I was sure that there would be something that I could fit into.

After she left the shower, I went in myself. Once again, it felt like my legs were too weak to support me, trembling under me as I stood in the shower. It made my lower lip wobble, and I bit down on it before I could start sobbing. I didn't know yet if it was the fear making me tremble, or if I was sick again.

I hurried, just in case, and got out with a towel wrapped around me, to find Jessi already dressed and waiting, with clothes laid out on the bed for me.

"I had some new underwear," she said, jumping up from the bed. "I don't know if it'll fit you too well but try it out. All the clothes are clean. I'll go make breakfast now, and you can tell me when you'd like to go, okay?"

I nodded slowly, watching her closely. My friend was frazzled and worried. Her body looked like it was trembling just as much as mine. She was fully dressed, but her hair still stuck up in places, and I wondered if she'd tried to tug on it in frustration. Her hands fluttered a bit in the air as if she wasn't sure what she was supposed to do with them, before she clasped them together in front of her so hard her knuckles went white.

"Meet me in the living room after you're done," she finally said, leaving me to get dressed.

Slowly, I pulled on the clothes she'd left for me. As I'd thought, they were all a little big, but they still fit. The underwear must have been a little small for her, which was probably why it was still new, and it didn't feel uncomfortable at all. I sat down on the bed for a few minutes to catch my breath.

Don't be scared, I thought to myself. It could still be nothing.

I tried to encourage myself not to back down from this, because if the illness was back, I knew I'd have to be strong, even with Jessi there to help me.

By the time I moved to the front room, Jessi was finishing up on breakfast.

"Please, sit," she said, pointing to the small dining table. "The food is all done now."

I went silently to sit down and ate whatever she put in front of me. I would have to fast before surgery, but that wasn't going to be today, and I was feeling hungrier than I'd been in days.

Breakfast was a quiet affair, and I hated it because it was nothing like us. We usually chatted about everything and anything. When we finished, Jessi silently got up to take the dishes to the sink and washed them all before coming back to join me.

"When exactly… do you…" she hesitated.

I sighed, moving to get up. "We might as well head out now. The sooner I get this over with, the better. My doctor agreed to see me when I went back as soon as she had the time, so there's no point putting it off."

Jessi let out a shaky sigh.

"Okay," she said, getting up.

We picked up my coat, phone, and purse on our way out. Jessi was so distracted she almost forgot her key card inside. The trip down to the lobby was quiet, and we slipped out the staff entrance to where she'd parked her car. She unlocked it and we both got in.

"Which hospital?" she asked.

"Just drive, I'll give you the directions."

The car ride was as silent as we'd been the whole morning, broken now and then by my voice as I gave her the directions. I kept sneaking glances at her, and I felt bad to see her so distressed. She tried to hide it, putting up a strong front for my sake, but she was my closest friend, and I could read her well.

It was still pretty early by the time we got there, but I knew how early my doctor got into work. Jessi parked the car and we went into the hospital with me taking the lead.

My legs seemed to slow down the further we went like I was trying to put off the inevitable. We made it, and I stopped in front of my doctor's office. Jessi came to a stop beside me.

"Is this it?" she asked hesitantly.

I nodded, and with a deep breath, knocked.

"Come in, come in," called a familiar voice.

I hesitated as I opened the door and walked in, holding it open for Jessi to follow me in.

"Ah! Laura, you're here." Her eyes traveled to Jessi. "And you brought a…"

"Friend," I finished for her. "This is Jessi. Jessi, this is Dr. Matthew."

"I'm glad to see you're coming with someone for once," she said chidingly.

I shrugged helplessly. "I never thought I'd need to have someone else come with me. They're only tests."

Dr. Matthew gave me a disapproving look. Jessi nudged my shoulder, and when I looked over at her, she was giving me the same look.

"Well, anyway. Jessi, I'm glad to meet you," she said, holding out her hand.

"Likewise," Jessi said, shaking the doctor's hand. "Thank you for looking after my friend for this long. If she'd told me before she came to the hospital so often, I would have come earlier."

Dr. Matthew gave Jessi an approving look before she turned to me.

"Let's head into the examination room. Do you need me to go through the procedures?"

I shook my head slowly and followed her as she walked into the room attached to her office. I shot a last, almost desperate look at Jessi before the door closed behind us.

"Now," my doctor started. "Did you do the assignment I asked you to do last time?"

"I did," I said quietly.

She waited as I lifted up my arm and pointed, too scared to touch. She gave me a sympathetic look and stepped closer to me.

"Take off your coat, please, and sit on the examination table."

I did as instructed then raised my arm once more without being told. She looked off to the side with a frown as she felt the area I'd pointed to. Then she had me raise my other arm and gave that area the same attention. Finally, she felt both areas at the same time. I kept my eyes on her face, waiting for a change in her expression, but she kept it blank this time. She frowned when she came into contact with what I'd found.

"It's good that you found it," she said. "I only caught traces of it in your last test. This is not an ordinary lump."

That wasn't very encouraging, but I knew she wouldn't be. She wasn't the type to lie or give false hope, and I both liked and disliked that trait. I knew if I'd never had cancer before and she'd caught it, she wouldn't be as alarmed and would have given some words of encouragement. But because it wasn't my first time, it increased the chances of the lump I found being a cancerous cell.

"This is something we have to worry about," she said with a sigh, pulling back. "I wasn't sure when I looked you over last time. You've had years of being cancer free, so I'd hoped… but we need to get this lump investigated."

She pulled her gloves off and tossed them into the trash, then waited for me to put on my coat and follow her to where Jessi was still waiting. She hadn't even sat down, she looked like she'd been pacing around the room. She looked up when we both walked in, and at my bleak expression, her face fell.

"We need to have some tests done," Dr. Matthew said. "Please sit down, and I'll explain some things to you."

My body shook even more as I moved to one of the seats opposite the doctor at her desk. Jessi had to hold me by the arms to help me down into it. I didn't want further tests because I knew they'd hurt. Also, it was pretty much a confirmation that my ordeal had begun once again.

Jessi took the seat closest to me and reached for me to pull me into her arms. Having her comfort was such a blessing, and I stopped acting strong. I broke down crying and Dr. Matthew, wonderful woman that she was, let me have my time to cry as she put in orders for all the tests that I would need in the near, uncertain future.

MASON

I frowned at my phone as the line rang once again, and she refused to fucking answer it. I'd been trying to reach Laura for days and I still wasn't getting an answer. There were times when her phone would be off and the call would go straight to voicemail. Then there were times when my call got cut off or was just left to ring out.

"What the fuck is going on?" I asked aloud, feeling irritation creep up on me.

I didn't want to be irritated with Laura. She might have a good reason for ignoring me. She had promised me she wouldn't run, and I'd told her I trusted her. The problem was, now I felt as if the words had fallen on deaf ears because she'd done a disappearing act.

Fuck!

I couldn't deal with this. I'd had enough drama with my family, I didn't need it with my love life too.

A light ding made me look up, and I remembered I was

in the elevator. The doors had just opened to the office floor, and I stepped out, headed for the office. I gave the secretary a distracted nod of acknowledgment and let myself in. Trent looked up from his desk.

"You could knock, you know," he said, though he didn't look angry.

It wasn't like I'd ever knocked, and even if he told me to start doing it, I wouldn't get used to it. I was used to walking into this office, no matter who sat behind the desk.

"Sorry," I said distractedly, putting my phone and both my hands in my pants pockets. I shook my head at the idea of apologizing, I never did that.

Trent's eyebrows jumped up. "Wow, did you apologize to me? Mason, that's not like you."

He wasn't playing, and I wasn't in the fucking mood. A genuine note of worry entered his tone, and I was surprised to hear it. Trent and I weren't exactly close after all, no matter how friendly we acted with each other.

"Just..." I hesitated before deciding it would be better not to tell him just yet. Fuck, I hated the way I was talking like some kinda wimp or something as if I wasn't sure of myself and I didn't know if there was a problem. I still hadn't decided how I was going to break the news to my family. I was still planning the proposal, and I was thinking of telling them after that.

Of course, I needed to speak to Laura before any of that could happen.

"Just... what?"

I sighed. "Nothing important. I just don't feel like work today."

"Is it woman trouble?" he asked, and I stopped in my tracks wondering whether to tell him the truth, but I felt the need to talk to someone and that someone just happened to be him.

"Yeah, how did you guess?"

He shrugged, leaning back in his seat and crossing his arms. "You could say I'm in a similar predicament, though I don't know what exactly your problem is."

He was being smug about it, which put me off telling him the whole story. I'm dating one of the maids from the hotel. We've been dating for weeks already, and I think I'm in love with her. But right now, she's avoiding me, and I haven't got a clue why. Shit, back in the day it would have been the other way around. I would have given out my number after being too drunk and tried to let the girl down gently, but there was never a gentle way to break someone's heart, was there?

Maybe this was fucking karma?

All the times that I'd treated women badly and now there was this one woman. Someone who had plucked at my heart and now I was so fucking lost, and I felt the need to talk to someone about it. But I wasn't about to pour my heart out to Trent. I wasn't that fucking desperate.

"What's your problem? You're never interested in anything that's bothering me and now you want to act as if you're my best friend," I blurted, wanting to make sure that before I told him anything else, I was doing it with a clear conscious.

He sighed, and before I could say stop words were pouring out of his mouth. "Well, I wanted to ask her to move in with me, but she's still pretty reluctant. But then she asked for my help for a place to stay; only she wants to stay there with a friend of hers who's ill. I'm helping them out with the rent for a month, it might be longer than that but we'll see later. I don't mind any of that, but my problem is she doesn't have time to even pick up my calls, and I don't want to bother either of them by calling…"

A frown grew on his face as he stared off into space.

"Anyway, that's how it is. I can only be patient and wait for her to reach out to me because she's busy with her friend right now."

I hummed, wondering if this could be the reason Laura wasn't responding to me. Maybe she had something else keeping her distracted?

"I'm not sure if that could be it, but she's not picking up my calls…" I said with a hint of a whine that I didn't like at all.

"It could be anything. Just don't jump to any conclusions before you talk to her, or you might be wrong and end up regretting it." He sounded like he was talking from experience.

"Fine," I muttered. "I'll take your advice. But…"

"I'll assume you came here to ask for time off," he said, cutting me off. "Usually, I wouldn't. And you shouldn't be asking either, but we can't have you distracted or that could just cause a disaster later. You can go, and I'll pick up the slack for you, as long as you know you'll be making up the work later."

I snorted. "Why do you make it sound like homework?"

Still, I sent him a grateful smile as I left the office. I knew he wasn't kidding, and later I'd be annoyed with myself for it, but the most important thing was to find Laura. I'd been to her apartment already, and she hadn't been there both times I stopped by, so I went back to my room to call the cleaning department and ask about her.

"Hello, Margaret?" I spoke before she could say anything. "I'd like you to look into one of the maids for me. Laura? Is she around? Could you ask her to come to my room, please?"

I was being a little bold. I didn't even make the pretense that I was calling her up to come clean, and the other end of the call was silent for a long minute. But then I cleared my throat, and she seemed to come back to herself.

"Uh, Laura. I know her. I'm afraid she's not in today. She hasn't been in for some time, and I had someone else assigned to your room already."

I frowned, suddenly feeling worried. It was one thing for her not to be in her apartment or picking up her calls. I'd told myself she was either just not there when I went—though one time I'd waited in front of her door for an hour, and another time I went earlier than she usually left, in case I was just missing her—or she was staying with a friend. But if she wasn't coming into work, then I didn't even have a way to check in on her to see how she was doing.

"Why hasn't she been coming into work?" I asked.

She hesitated, but in the end, told me what I needed to know.

"The last time I spoke to her, she asked to take some time off. She didn't give me a straight reason why just said it was for health reasons. I didn't pry into what it was though, and I don't have anything more to tell you on the matter."

Health reasons... no way.

"Thank you for the information," I said distractedly, then set the phone down.

Slowly, I walked over to the couch and sat down in a daze. There was this uncomfortable feeling in my stomach like I'd just been gutted.

Health reasons... I knew, though she hadn't said it outright, that she'd had cancer before. With the little info I knew about cancer patients, I knew it was a possibility for them to relapse. If she had gone off the grid and even taken time out of work... Had it come back?

"Don't think that way," I muttered to myself, trying to push back the worry and fear wanting to overtake me. "It could be something else."

I didn't believe that though, and as I pulled my phone from my pocket to dial my sister, my hands trembled so much it took me a few tries before I managed. I held the phone up, the sound of my heart beating so loudly in my ears making me wonder if I would even hear her.

She answered on the second ring and I felt as if my heart skipped a fucking beat. Shit, I really was being a bit too sensitive these days. I'd gone from being angry all the time to a lovesick teenager and I thought about the saying, 'Love makes you do crazy things' and I started to believe it was true.

"What's up, Mason?" she chirped. "Do you want me to give you more pointers about your girlfriend?"

That had me squeezing my eyes shut. That pretty much meant she didn't know anything about Laura, right? But I decided to ask anyway.

"You said the two of you were friends," I mumbled, my voice sounding very far away. "Emily, have you heard from Laura? She isn't picking up any of my calls. She's not home and I just heard she took time off work for health reasons. If you know anything, please, I need to talk to her."

My heart beat anxiously as I waited for her answer, even though I already guessed what it would be and that I would be disappointed.

After a long moment of silence, she answered, and I felt strangely relieved.

"I… don't know. I'm sorry, Mason. I told you, I don't speak to her as often as I speak to Jessi. She's always busy, so I try not to bother her too often."

I sighed and leaned back, tilting my head against the back of the couch as I let my eyes slide closed. Fuck. If even Emily had no idea, then how could I find her?

"If she is sick and ignoring you right now, you know you can't use that as an excuse to leave her, right?"

"I don't need you to tell me that," I retorted.

"I think you do," she said. "If she's pushing you away right now, it's not because she doesn't want to see you. If it's so important that she had to take time off work, she's probably scared right now, and she's only doing this to protect you. So don't abandon her, okay?"

I winced, squeezing my eyes closed and felt like something pierced my chest. I'd meant it when I said I didn't need her to tell me. I wasn't about to just leave Laura. The only way that would happen is if she told me to my face she wanted me gone, and she hadn't done that yet.

"I don't plan on it," I promised. "So don't worry about that."

"Keep waiting, and you'll hear from her at some point," she said. "This is going to be the decider of your relationship, to see just how serious you are. If she is sick, do you think you can love her, and be there for her for what she needs? This is probably the thought going through her mind, and why she's avoiding you. Can you be her caretaker, her friend, and her lover at a time like this?"

30

MASON

Shit. Emily was making sense and I realized that as much as she kept telling me that she was all grown up, I'd never given her credit for it, because she was talking like a woman with a strong head on her shoulders. Sure, she acted every bit like Daddy's little princess, but I knew better. I usually forgot that unlike me she usually surrounded herself with people who lived very different lives from the members of our family. I'd always reprimanded her for it, no matter how jokingly it was done, but it had made her so much wiser than the rest of us.

Her words rang true in my mind, body, and soul, and they left me both overwhelmed and speechless at the same time. It was as if I didn't understand myself anymore and no longer did I feel the need to try and put up a front and pretend to be an arrogant pig. I didn't have anything to prove anymore. I was human like everybody else.

"I'm going to let you go now," Emily said after a long moment of silence. "But please, think things over carefully, all right? Don't make a decision now that you could come to regret in the future."

She cut off the call, and I was grateful because I didn't think I could find the words. My hand dropped to my lap and I swallowed the sudden lump in my throat. My eyes stung, and I blinked them several times. I couldn't remember the last time I'd cried, and it wasn't going to be now.

I was worried. Could I bring myself to do all that? Possibly for the rest of my life? Because even if it was cancer again, and she returned to normal health after that, the risk would always be there.

Shit.

Suddenly, I felt restless. There was no point in just sitting there feeling sorry for myself, so I jumped up. I went to take my car keys and hurried out of my room. I headed for the elevator and pressed the button, then waited impatiently for the doors to open. I was just about to go looking for the stairs when the door opened, and as soon as I let myself inside, I regretted it.

Should have just gone for the stairs.

I wasn't claustrophobic but being in the enclosed space with all the nervous energy running through my body made me uneasy. It was made even worse because I was alone. The walls of the elevator were reflective, and I could see what my expression looked like. Before it could make me break down, I looked at my feet, leaning back with my hands on the bars against the walls, holding myself steady.

When the doors opened again in the lobby, I practically stumbled out. I ignored the curious looks of the people waiting for the elevator, and others milling around the lobby. I kept my gaze on the ground, hoping no one would stop me to ask what was wrong with me, though that was probably a tall order.

I made it to my car and got inside. I waited a moment to catch my breath, trying to settle myself before I started the car and drove. I headed right for the house I'd called up to buy the day after I saw it, so I wouldn't miss my chance with it and have it sold out from under me. I still wanted Laura's input on it, so I would only make a clean purchase afterward.

The drive was shorter because I was driving faster, and I parked my car against the curb, then jumped out. I had a key to the house, and I kept it on the same ring as my car key and remote.

I let myself inside, through the fence and up the drive to the front door. I unlocked it and walked inside. I'd been coming here pretty often since I rented it, and I'd made some changes. The furniture had already been brought in, and I'd had some guys come in and do the paint. I'd put in a lot of Laura's favorite colors. I thought it looked good enough that it didn't need to be improved anywhere besides making it livable, and I'd done that.

When I looked at it before, I couldn't help but feel proud. I thought she'd fall in love with the house just like I did, that she'd accept and move in with me happily in this house we could make into our home. Looking at it all once again though, I could only find glaring problems.

All of it was what I wanted, what I thought Laura would want. I'd put in everything that would be to her taste, but the reality was that Laura didn't have any actual choice in any of it. It was still me doing whatever I wanted and hoping Laura would go along with it.

I've done it again, I thought to myself with a sigh.

I'd thought I was getting better, that I was making things better between us. I wasn't just doing what I wanted on my own; I had her in mind all the time. But I didn't always include her, and I hadn't with this house. I'd hoped it would be a surprise, but I'd been so worried it would sell because how could no one else fall in love with it just like I had? Then I'd been too excited and started planning what the inside would look like, and went ahead with it instead of waiting to plan it all with Laura. If she hadn't liked how it turned out, I would have gladly changed whatever she didn't like, but… that didn't change my mistake.

"Dammit," I cursed, only instead of being angry with myself, I was feeling subdued.

Without even meaning to, I'd taken control because I was so used to having it, even knowing Laura didn't like it. Even when I disliked it when it came to my dad treating me that way. It didn't change just because Laura and I were dating, and I loved her enough to do all this for her. For all his meddling, I knew Dad cared for me. His methods just annoyed me, and I hated that Laura had probably felt the same way with me.

Once again… I'd all but shown the woman I loved that her taste wasn't good enough.

I walked over to the living room and sat down on the couch. It was large and comfortable, and I'd pictured us cuddling together in it under an afghan, watching a movie together. I didn't have a TV installed yet, but I'd had plans to.

"Laura," I said out loud. "You… would forgive me if I said I'm sorry, right? You're not just going to stop talking to me and not see me again… you'll be coming back…"

No one answered, and I didn't expect it from an empty house, but it still left my chest feeling heavy. I tilted my head back, squeezed my eyes closed, and even covered them with my hand, pressing hard enough for it to be uncomfortable. My eyes were stinging again, and I tried to hold it back but I couldn't.

For the first time in my adult life, since before I hit high school even, I cried.

At first, it was just a small tear slipping out the corner of one eye. I felt it as it slowly trickled down the side of my face, wet and warm. More followed after it, and I lost all hope of controlling them. My breathing and heartbeat picked up, and noises I hadn't made since the last time I cried to my mother when I was a kid left my mouth. I tried to muffle them. The hand over my eyes moved to cover my mouth, but they still slipped out.

Shit.

It was pathetic that I was sitting by myself in an empty house and crying. But what else could I do? I couldn't find Laura. She'd even moved out of her apartment, so she didn't want to be found. Even worse, she could be very sick, and here I was crying like a baby.

I should move, I tried to tell myself. Wherever she is, she probably needed me. I should go to her.

But I couldn't bring myself to move. I couldn't even

open my eyes because I knew Laura wouldn't be there and seeing it would just make me cry more. I choked out a laugh, thinking how surprised they'd be, all those people who thought they knew me. I came off as confident, but it was just something I'd learned to project because of Dad.

I couldn't be confident anymore, not when it came to Laura. Already, the worst-case scenarios were running through my mind.

If she was sick, then she was probably going to the hospital. I'd read up a little on breast cancer since she and I got together, and I knew even just the tests were painful, let alone going through the treatments. I thought back to what Emily had said to me and wondered if I could go through with it.

Laura would be in a lot of pain, and she'd need a lot of help. She'd also need me to be by her side to give her comfort. I'd have to sit there and watch her be in pain. I'd have to live with the uncertainty that cancer might not go away this time.

Was she going to have surgery? Had she gone through the tests already, and how painful had it been? Would she need chemotherapy? How long would it all take? All those questions I couldn't answer kept running through my mind, and I had no answer for any of them. Neither did I know whether I wanted the answer, in case they were favorable. There was nothing in this situation that I could have control over, and that was just even more heartbreaking.

Behind all those thoughts was the one I feared most.

The one I wanted to ignore and pretend it could never be a possibility, but I knew better.

What was I going to do if this was fatal? If even after going through the treatments… Laura died. Could I cope with that?

The thought just made me cry more, and my other hand clutched my chest because my heart ached at the mere thought of it.

Laura couldn't die yet. I hadn't even had the chance to love her properly yet! I hadn't told her I loved her. But I had no control over any of it, and that was perhaps the thought that hurt the most.

31

LAURA

"Are you sure about this?" Jessi asked me once again.

I sighed, my head lolling on the seat's headrest. I wasn't sure, and that was the problem. There was no point in running away, was there? If I was honest, I was grateful to both Jessi and Trent. Trent for renting the house close enough to the hospital, and her for staying there with me, and taking time off as well when she didn't need to.

It was time now. I'd finished all my tests which was strange because at the time I'd felt that they'd never end and now they were done, it felt as if the time had passed so quickly. One thing was for sure: I was exhausted. As much as I would love to stick with Jessi until I had to go back to the doctor, there was a part of me that would rather be alone in my little apartment, if only for a little bit.

"You really don't need to worry," I said wondering if I was reassuring her or myself. I hated being a burden to anyone. "I'll be fine… some alone time would do me good." I realized what I really needed, it wasn't so much to not feel as if I was a burden, it was just some time to be alone.

"And you're sure you're okay?" she asked, double-checking.

I sighed and faced my friend to give her a wan smile. "You don't have to worry too much. I feel better now than I have for the past few days. I just want to sleep in my bedroom, surrounded by my favorite things and wait for morning and knit something. God, you don't know how much I miss knitting!" And I didn't know exactly how it would change, the thing that scared me.

"You're like a grandma before your time. You're obsessed with knitting!"

We both laughed. I thought about knitting, but the truth of the matter was that I was too weak to really do it at the moment. Knitting calmed me and made me feel whole, but it took too much concentration at times.

She undid her seatbelt and reached for me with open arms. I leaned in for a long, comforting hug. I almost lost the fight with my tears but kept my head tilted up and blinked until I didn't think I was going to cry again. I'd cried enough in front of my friend already. I knew just how much she hated seeing me in pain, and I wouldn't make her see any more. With all the support she'd already given me, it was more than enough.

After I went to see Dr. Matthew… well, I might need more comfort afterward so I could at least let her relax and see her boyfriend. She'd completely put him off while she was with me, and I didn't want him to have such a low impression of me before we even officially met.

"It's fine, really," I said when I felt the hug was going on too long. "You have a date, don't you? You need to get home and freshen up before going to meet your boyfriend."

She sighed as she pulled back, settling into her seat and putting on her seatbelt again.

"I wouldn't call it a date, exactly. He's taking the day off and I'm just going to his place. You are right though, I'll probably take a shower first," she conceded.

"Go and make a date of it then," I said, my smile growing a little brighter. "You have such a wonderful boyfriend, and you've been in love with him for years. You can't just neglect him."

"It's not neglect," she retorted, frowning. "I'm taking care of you, and you're my best friend. Trent understands and if he didn't then I wouldn't be with him. I can't deal with being in a relationship and having to be someone I'm not. I want to be myself and comfortable being me. I am with Trent, so it's all good."

I sighed. "Thank you, Jessi, for being my very best friend. And I'm glad things are working out well for you and Trent. Also, thank you for looking after me, but I'll be fine for a few hours alone. Just… enjoy your time together, at least. Even if it's only for my sake."

Her frown only grew deeper.

"I've kept you long enough," I said, because I had a feeling if I didn't try to leave first, I'd end up crying in front of her, and she wouldn't go. This whole thing had been my idea to begin with, I couldn't just allow her to keep ignoring Trent. That wasn't fair to either of them.

"Should I come pick you up?" Her voice was shaking, and I knew that she was nervous about asking after I just told her that I needed 'me' time.

I bit my lip, unsure. I'd been thinking of Mason lately and feeling a little guilty at how much I was ignoring him. I wasn't sure if I could muster the courage to contact him after so long… but when I was sending Jessi off to her boyfriend, this had been the plan. I'd told her I had someone I could ask, but to keep her phone on because I wasn't sure I could go through with it.

There had been so many calls and messages from Mason, and I'd evaded them all up to now. It hadn't been easy for me, a few times I almost caved. Now though, I didn't want to avoid him anymore. Having Jessi around was a blessing, but…

I missed him.

"It's fine," I said. "I'll call you if I need you, but if I don't, just spend time with Trent. If I don't see you again today, I promise to give you an update after I see the doctor."

She still looked reluctant, but she sighed and started the car again. We'd been sitting out there for nearly twenty minutes, and I reached for the door handle.

"Fine," she said, resigned. "But I swear, Laura, if you don't call or message me by tonight, I will come looking for you."

"That's fine. I'll see you later, Jessi. And thanks again."

I opened the door and climbed out. The air was a bit chilly, and my shoulders rose around my ears as I shivered from a cold breeze, holding my coat tighter around my body. I waved at Jessi as she started the car, then watched as she drove away.

Once her car was out of sight, I turned and walked into my building. It was an old place, not like some of the newer, more luxurious looking apartment buildings in the area. I felt a sense of nostalgia as I closed the creaky door behind me and headed for the steep staircase. I was in no hurry, going up the steps slowly. I'd meant it when I said I was in my best condition over the past few days, but I still felt a little bit weak.

I came to a stop in front of my front door and waited a long moment just staring at it before I let myself inside.

Nothing had changed since the last time I was there. I'd cleaned up before I left, but there was a slight musty smell hanging in the room.

"First of all," I muttered to myself. "Open up the windows."

My whole apartment only had two proper windows. There was a third, but that was a tiny one in the bathroom so I didn't usually count it. If I opened the one in my bedroom, I might sleep and forget to close it. Spending my short nap freezing was the last thing I wanted to do. So I went to the kitchen and opened that window as far as it would go. It wouldn't matter too much if I forgot to close it before I slept because my apartment was several floors up.

I took a glass of water, then looked through my fridge before I remembered there was nothing left in it. Not even in the cupboards. I'd already eaten, Jessi had made sure of that, but a snack might be enough to take my mind off things. I was alone now, just like I'd wanted. I didn't feel rested at all. But I didn't think I could go to sleep if I tried.

In an hour or so, I would be getting the results from all that testing, and it would be the decider of what my life would be like going forward. If the cancer wasn't gone then I was in trouble. If it was then I could only rejoice. Just thinking that my life hedged on a piece of paper... it was enough to drive me crazy.

So, now that I was alone, what should I do? Even though I'd insisted on being alone, I had no idea. I'd figured I would just go to my room, lie down on my bed and sleep the time away with an alarm on my phone to remind me. My doctor wouldn't even mind if I was a little later, as long as it wasn't longer than an hour. But when I walked into the bedroom, all I could do was stare at my bed. I didn't think I could fall asleep. I felt too restless for that.

Maybe listen to music? Or watch TV? Probably not, because I'd be tempted to put on some melodramatic songs that would just lead me to cry, and TV didn't always catch my interest much. I didn't even feel in the mood to read online.

"Knitting," I said to myself. I could always do some knitting to keep my mind occupied; maybe I could do a little, not as much as I used to, but maybe a little would do me some good. It was the one thing that always managed to make me feel calm, after all.

I walked into my bedroom and picked up my last knitting project. I stiffened a little when I realized I could be knitting something for me to use later on, but I shook that thought off quickly. I relocated to the living room and sat down on the couch with a sigh.

I arranged my hands and the knitting needles, but I couldn't even start because my hands were trembling. I let go of the needles, staring at my trembling hands like it was the first time I'd noticed, feeling a little betrayed.

Before I could pick them back up and try again, there was a knock on the door. It was enough to make me pause, wondering who it could be. It was probably Jessi coming back to check on me one more time but there was force behind that knock, whoever was on the other side of the door was stronger than Jessi.

Could it be…?

My heart went still, then started beating very quickly. When the knocking came again, I started with a gasp. And then, his voice.

"Laura!" he called through the door. "I can see the light is on, so you have to be in there! Please, Laura, let me in!"

Mason… how long had it been since I'd last heard his voice? Too long, because it was making my heart waver, even as loud, obnoxious, and desperate as it sounded. I realized right then that I would have copped out of calling him, but he'd come to me instead.

After some hesitation, I got up, leaving my knitting to the side.

"Laura!" he yelled some more. "Let me in! I swear I will make a scene on your doorstep until you open this door!"

That was enough to bring a smile to my lips, a shaky one, as my eyes stung. The ever-unflappable Mason Thompson, screaming like a lunatic at my door.

With my doubts gone, I took sure steps to the door and opened it. He froze with his fist in the air, like he'd been about to deliver another harsh round of knocking.

I'd hated him, I'd loved him. But right then, I needed someone that wasn't Jessi, not after what she'd already sacrificed because of me. I just needed a friend, and there he stood.

"Mason."

LAURA

I didn't even think about it, I just threw myself at him, wrapping my arms tight around his waist and holding on as I thought about how selfish I'd been shutting him out. His eyes were red as if he hadn't slept. He wasn't wearing a suit and he wasn't clean shaven like he always was. I knew that the stress and tiredness had been a result of me and all I wanted was to have him hold me in his arms.

"Mason," I repeated his name, my voice hushed as I started to get emotional.

My eyes squeezed closed, and my throat grew tight and itchy. Tentatively, he circled his arms around me, and just like that, I broke down.

"Whoa! Laura, what is it? What's wrong? What's going on? Tell me..."

Immediately, Mason was firing questions at me, sounding worried. He rubbed circles into my back with one hand, carded the fingers of his other hand through my hair, doing it ever so gently.

"I'm sorry for ignoring you," I said through my sobs as I buried my face into his chest. "So sorry!"

Seeing him in the flesh after so long, there was no point in denying it to myself. I hadn't wanted to see him because I knew seeing me in pain would bring him pain too, and I hadn't wanted that. The idea of breaking things off with him, even though it would have been better for him in the long run, had only left me feeling cold. I would have done it for his sake, but I would have hated it.

"No, it's okay. I understand," Mason murmured, burying his face in my hair. "I was worried, Laura. I figured you needed time, and I gave it to you. I'm a pretty impatient guy and insensitive at times. Things weren't working on my terms and I wanted to be in control of it. I wanted to make sure that you were okay."

He paused, and I could tell he'd done something, but I couldn't figure out what, until he revealed he'd been coming here every night since he found out that I was too sick to go to work.

His explanation had me wailing louder, and even with my face pressed against his chest, it wasn't so muffled that the sound didn't carry down the hall.

Mason cursed. "Fuck, I didn't mean to. I meant… shit. Why am I so fucking insensitive?"

I didn't think I could stop myself, so I didn't even try to.

Mason put his hands on the tops of my arms to push me back. I went willingly because I deserved it if he wasn't going to forgive me for leaving him out of the loop for so long. But he was only doing it so there was enough space between us for him to lean down and pick me up bridal style, then walk me into the apartment. My arms automatically wrapped around his neck as I buried my face into his chest once more.

He carried me in his arms as he locked the door, then walked us further into the room. There was the sound of another door opening and closing, and he sat us both down on the bed with me in his lap. It had me feeling a little embarrassed, so I tried to get off, but he wrapped an arm around my waist to keep me there.

After a good long cry, I started to calm down a little. The tears didn't stop but at least I was no longer sobbing. Mason moved under me, and when I opened my eyes to know what he was trying to do, I saw him holding a handkerchief up for me. That just made me even more choked up, and I wiped my tears and blew my nose into it.

"Laura…" he started, but he didn't sound like his usual self. He sounded like he was hesitating.

Just like that, I spilled everything.

"I told you I had breast cancer," I blurted out. "Years ago, when I was in college. I didn't even know at first, I just felt something on my chest that was off, but I didn't think too much about it. A while later, I started feeling off, and when I fainted in class one too many times, I decided to go to a doctor for a checkup."

Mason stayed quiet, and very still, letting me get it all off of my chest.

"When they diagnosed me with cancer, I was so scared, Mason. I barely had any money, I was putting myself through college with a part-time job and my parents' inheritance, which I only got after I'd turned eighteen. They started telling me about all these tests I would have to take, talking about surgery and chemotherapy. I didn't have any family, and I didn't tell my friends about any of it."

I stopped to blow my nose again and wipe up some more tears. Mason's broad hand was rubbing up and down my spine, as I quieted down to sniffling.

Mason whispered, "I know. Call me paranoid, but when I met you I did some reading up so I knew some of what you went through."

"I went through all of it, and somehow managed to pay for it. Then I got better and I moved here. I've been going to the doctor regularly, and recently, they caught something."

His body went still against me as he sucked in a sharp breath, his hand stopping its movement, and I squirmed in his lap until he continued.

"What…"

He hesitated to ask, but I guessed already what he wanted to know now, and I sighed.

"I went through some testing. I'm waiting on the results. I have to go to my doctor's office in like half an hour. I don't know how it's going to go, but Mason, I'm scared."

With that admission, he sighed and wrapped both arms around me, holding me close.

"It's okay to be scared," he said, his voice quiet and

soothing. Then he chided, "You could have just come to me instead of hiding yourself away."

"I didn't hide. I stayed with a friend, my best friend. I just didn't want to be a burden to you," I explained but it sounded so weak as if I was excusing my behavior.

"I didn't know what to think. When you thought… it doesn't matter. You're okay now."

I bit my lip, feeling guilt wash over me.

"I know, I was selfish, but at the time it felt like the best decision," I confessed trying to think about what it would have felt like if it was the other way around. I would have hated him if he'd shut me out that way. But then I hadn't wanted to contact him. Not then, all I could think about was if I was going to die or not. I had to explain to him. Make him understand.

"I've been through all this before and it's not pretty."

I moved away from him so he'd understand what I was trying to say for both our sakes.

"You couldn't handle it. At times, I don't even know how to handle it. I see them in the clinics, in the hospitals. Partners with their husbands, wives, girlfriends. And it is not just the cancer they're trying to deal with, but with their partner. They come to see them and hold back their tears as they watch their partner in agony. They hold their hand and all they want to do is take their pain away, but they can't. We've been together a little while, but not that long and I couldn't deal with the responsibility of watching you see me go through this." I said it and I felt proud about admitting what was really going through my mind at the time.

"I know a little bit about cancer, and I know it can be long and painful. If my own money isn't enough, then I'll borrow more from my family, but I'm getting you the best care, and I will never, not once, leave you alone, okay?"

This was the Mason I was used to, high-handed and in control, even when he meant well. Only this time, it didn't annoy me as much as it usually did. Maybe I was coming around to the fact he might not change entirely, and I was somewhat okay with it.

"You know, I resented you once," I said. He arched his eyebrow, and I giggled. "Mostly way in the beginning, but every time you showed off it came back. You have it all, everything I needed back when I was ill, but couldn't afford, right at your fingertips. And while it would certainly be useful to have a boyfriend with the cash to get me through this, I have my savings, and I'm pretty good at looking after myself. I'm not with you for your money, Mason."

"I know—"

I put a finger to his lips to cut him off.

"Just let me finish. You having so much and me having so little was one of the reasons I didn't think you and I would be a good match, and if something ever happened between us, it couldn't possibly end happily. Your money is nice, Mason, but right now, all I need is a friend…"

I kept talking and talking until I wasn't even sure what I was saying. I knew I was rambling because my nerves were all frazzled, but I couldn't help it, and I spit everything out. I explained it all, my feelings, my worries, my terrors. My thought process in our relationship, my illness, our possible future, if we even had one. I didn't stop until it felt like I was going to pass out from not taking in enough air. And then I did run out of the air, stopping mid-sentence to take in big gulps of it, only I didn't know where I cut off, so I didn't bother to continue.

So instead, I looked up at him with huge, scared eyes, silently begging him for one thing. Sure, his money would be convenient, but if there was anything that would bring me peace of mind, it would be his presence.

Like he saw my silent question, his expression softened, and he ducked his head to press his lips against mine in a kiss, his arms tightening even more around me.

"Don't worry," he said. "I promise to always be there for you. For now, why don't you get ready and I'll take you to the doctor?"

33

MASON

I let Laura have her say and decided I had a few things of my own to say or I would explode. I could afford to give her the best treatment money can buy, but right now, she just wanted a friend and I was cool with that. They say money can't buy love, but it buys a lot of other things, and that includes the best healthcare. It's sad but true, and later I'd argue with her about it until she caved, because her health wasn't something I was willing to play with.

She looked hesitant, like she wanted to let me off the hook and I wasn't having it.

"You told me about partners and how the patients have to watch their loved ones suffering, but they never have to go through it themselves. That's why they cry for them and wish they could take away the pain. I can sit and hate the idea that you're going through so much pain, but I would never, ever in a million years understand it unless I contract cancer myself."

She slumped down and as she sat she said, "I wouldn't wish this on my worst enemy."

The idea of Laura having any enemies brought a smile to my face. She had no idea how beautiful she was on the inside as well as the outside.

"I'm going to be a fucking pain in the arse from now on, Laura. I promise you that. I'm going to make you think, 'Shut the fuck up Mason', but I don't care. I want the best for you and if I fucking cry in your arms, so be it. If I pay your bills and buy you treats, you're going to take them, because when I couldn't get hold of you and I didn't have a fucking clue if you were alive or dead, that was far worse than being by your side. Trust me. I will do whatever it takes to keep you by my side from now on, my love, and nothing can change that or push me away."

She pouted and she didn't even think about disputing what I said to her. She smiled in the end and kissed me before she got up and headed to the shower. I was dressed, but I'd made sure my phone was off.

The last thing I needed was my dramatic family calling. I watched as she re-entered the room a few minutes later and started to get dressed. Before she'd have been shy around me. Now, it seemed almost natural for her to be naked in front of me and I smiled at it. She knew I was right and she was slowly and surely starting to trust me.

She nodded. "Let's do this…"

Her voice was quivering, and I knew she was scared but she had no reason to be, because the whole time she was getting ready and dressed, I was praying. Me, Mason Thompson closed his eyes for a brief second and prayed for everything to be alright. It had to be. Laura came into my life for a reason, and it wasn't for her to leave just as fast as she'd come into it.

I stood up and said, "Great." I smiled with confidence knowing there was nothing to worry about. Then we walked out of the apartment and headed for my car. I still kept an eye on her in case she tried something silly like closing the door behind me and staying inside. So I made sure that she left first and I swiftly closed the door behind me. Laura listened to what I'd said and as she followed me to the car, I wrapped my arm around her waist and smiled. "It's going to be alright."

Again, she gently nodded as she sat down. This time I was sure she was smiling too.

"Which hospital is it?" I asked, putting on my seatbelt. "It should be in my GPS."

She told me the name of the hospital, and my GPS brought up the directions and it was time for us to leave. I started the car, following the directions, and we seemed to arrive in no time at all. I glanced over at Laura who was clutching at the seatbelt and shaking. I sighed.

"Come on, Laura," I encouraged. "You'll get the news at some point, so you might as well get it over with."

"But what if it's bad news?" she protested weakly.

"It won't be." I wanted it to be true too much to think otherwise. "If we hear something that we don't like then we'll get a second opinion. Either way, you're not doing this alone."

I kissed her hand and that small smile, the nervous one that agreed with me appeared on her face. I got out first and went around to the side, opening the door for her. I leaned inside to undo her seatbelt and crouched down as I took both of her hands in mine.

"Just come in with me, okay? I'll be with you the whole time if you'd like, and you can strangle my hand if it makes you feel better. Or my head?"

She laughed. "I can't strangle your head…"

"Oh, you've tried it then. That's why my head always feels funny in the morning."

It changed both of our moods as I hit the lock on the car, and we headed for the hospital building. I didn't know where exactly we were going, but Laura had clearly been there plenty of times. I was confused at the many turns we took, but she didn't even stop to ask or check the directions. Finally, we came to a corridor with some plastic seats up against the wall, to the side of a door, and she stopped. I checked the nameplate.

"Dr. Matthew?" I asked.

Laura nodded. "She's the doctor I've been seeing since I moved and started my routine visits here."

I looked to some seats where a few other people were clearly waiting to go inside themselves. Laura sat in the closest empty seat and I sat down next to her. Across from us, there was a little plastic case put up against the wall with some pamphlets inside. Because I was bored, I decided to pick up one to read.

Oncology, huh…

I started from the front, occasionally checking on Laura sitting next to me. I held the pamphlet with one hand, the other staying firmly in both of Laura's. By how tight she held me, it was obvious she was anxious about this. I learned more about oncology as we sat there waiting for her appointment.

"My sister, Emily, says you guys are friends. Does she know about this?"

She shook her head. Some part of me was relieved but also shocked that she didn't tell Emily. Relieved knowing that I wasn't the only person that she'd shut out and disappointed at the idea that Laura wanted to do this alone.

"You can tell her if you like?"

I was surprised about her offering for me to tell her friend, so I pulled out my phone. I didn't know if Emily had received any updates on her friend after the last time she and I talked, but she'd sounded genuinely worried when I asked her about Laura going off the grid.

Besides, I needed someone to be my help on the outside while I focused on being with Laura in that moment.

First of all, I looked up other doctors. Whatever result Laura got, I was going to make sure she got a second, maybe third or fourth opinion, just in case. I saved their contacts to my phone book. I'd be seeking them out later, but not with Laura right there or she might complain.

Next, I sent texts to my sister. I explained as much as I thought I could, that Laura was sick, that she'd done tests and was getting her results today. I also added that it was possibly cancer. Then I directed her to find out what Laura might need, in spite of the outcome of this appointment.

Last but not least, I sent messages to Dad. I would have sent them to his secretary, but as far as I knew he still wasn't going to the office, and I wondered if he'd just let

Trent take his position full time. Dad and I set up an appointment in his home office.

It was time. I needed to tell my dad about my intentions because I wasn't going to put it off after this. I'd put myself through the ringer worrying about what could possibly happen to Laura, and what our future could possibly be like when she was hiding from me. After my little cry at the house meant to be ours, I'd made a few resolutions, and I meant to stick to them.

Laura was the woman I wanted, and while we hadn't been dating all that long, I knew I wanted to marry her, ill or not, if she'd have me. After all the shit she'd had to go through, twice, I wanted the rest of her life to be magic, and I would definitely make sure of that. Her kind of magic, not mine.

I wasn't about to give up my money. Not only did I earn everything in my bank account, it wasn't my fault who I was born to, and I wasn't just going to reject it. I wasn't going to give up the job I did for Dad either, because not only did it help the family business and earn me a lot of cash per deal, I sometimes found it enjoyable, like a game where getting the deal was what determined a victory. I hadn't failed yet, and I planned to keep that up. But other than that, I'd give Laura whatever she wanted, even if all she ever wanted from me was my love and my presence. I had plenty of both to give her.

"Laura?"

I'd been so preoccupied, it took hearing my girlfriend's name being called to snap me out of my daze. I looked up to see a woman who was probably around the same age or slightly older than Laura, dressed in a lab coat, standing in front of the open office door and gazing at us.

"It's time," she said.

Laura stood up, keeping my hand in hers, and I followed immediately. We walked into the office, the doctor looking down at our hands in interest, but not mentioning anything. She closed the door behind us and went around to sit behind her desk, gesturing us to the two seats on the opposite side.

"Dr. Matthew, this is Mason," Laura introduced as we sat down.

"It's good to meet you, Mason," she said bluntly, picking up some papers from her desk. "I'm going to assume since you brought him along, that you don't mind him hearing the news?"

She looked to Laura with an arched eyebrow, and Laura nodded. I hadn't even realized I was worried, but I definitely relaxed when she didn't just ask me to leave the room.

"He's my boyfriend," she admitted.

That made my heart soar.

Dr. Matthew glanced at me. "In that case, I'm very glad to meet you. I'm going to need you to stick close to Laura for a long while because she's going to need you."

Laura's hand tightened around mine. "Then... is..."

The doctor smiled as she held one of the papers for Laura to take. Slowly, without releasing my hand, she reached for the piece of paper. She trembled, but no one in the room mentioned it, and she brought it closer so we could read it.

"You got lucky," Dr. Matthew declared before we could see the contents. "What you have under your arm is a benign lymphoma. The symptoms of a benign lymphoma are very similar to the cancerous lymphoma, but there is a huge difference."

"And by your smile, I'm assuming this is good news?" Laura hesitantly asked the question we were both wondering about.

"That is correct, Laura. Their symptoms are similar, but their effects are different. The benign lymphoma, for one, is not as deadly. The number of patients dying from it is so much less, as long as it's treated early. And the good news for you is that they are easily cured."

There was a long silence as everyone in the room let those words sink in. Then I felt Laura's hand tighten around mine, and when I glanced over at her, I noticed her lips were trembling.

"You are going to need surgery," Dr. Matthew continued. "It's a good thing that it was found pretty early as you'll need to have it removed. Just like cancerous lymphoma, it can spread. At the moment, from what the tests say, it's small enough that you won't even need to have to undergo radiation therapy again. You will still be coming for checkups in the weeks afterward, but after the surgery, you should have a clean bill of health."

I didn't know how much more strength Laura could have, but she took my advice from before to heart, and absolutely strangled my hand. I let her, reaching with my other arm to pull her to me because I could see she was about to lose it. She sunk into me, and I absorbed her into my arms readily, glancing over at the doctor.

"Thank you so much, Dr. Matthew," I said fervently. "How soon do you think she can have the surgery?"

"I wanted to clear it with Laura before I set a date."

Laura pulled herself together just long enough to talk to the doctor, and she also left me with some instructions. We waited for the surgery appointment, and once we had that, we left.

The whole way back in the car, it was me holding her hand tightly.

"When we get back," I said, my voice low. "I am taking you to your room and I am going to make love to you for the rest of the day. No getting out of bed, Laura. Any objections?"

I glanced over at her, to find her beaming at me.

"No objection at all."

34

MASON

Fuck, I was so fucking happy. My life was really moving in the right direction. At first, I'd been angry all the time. When I was a kid growing up, I'd looked up to my aloof older half-brother, to an extent, and I'd also looked up to Dad. Until my older brother left, and suddenly Dad expected me to fill his shoes when I didn't want to. Dad making me give up my passion and love for rugby in high school had been the last straw for me, and though I'd hidden it all perfectly, I was angry. I was a partier too. It was the coping mechanism I'd picked to help with the resentment I felt toward my dad and my brother.

However, I wasn't constantly angry or that much of a partier anymore. And I didn't think I'd be going back to that kind of life in the near or far off future.

So I felt it was the best time to invite Dad over to our new house, where I'd already moved in, then convinced Laura to move in with me as well—not that it was hard because she fell for it just like I did as soon as she saw it. I was out in the front yard when Dad's car pulled up. He and Mom got out, and she pressed a quick kiss to my cheek before running off with excitement to see her baby's new house. I'd already sold off my old place and used the proceeds to make the full purchase of the new house, and I'd put the deed in both mine and Laura's names.

"So this is your new place," Dad said as he looked where Mom had gone off to, then looked around the yard and the neighborhood. "It's quiet. Not too far from the city, and not too close either. It's good."

I smiled wryly. "As much as I'm grateful for your approval, it doesn't matter in the long run. I only called you here because there's something I wanted you to know. I would have told you before…"

"I had to cancel the earlier meeting because something important came up."

"This is important, too," I said. But I moved on quickly. I wasn't trying to pick a fight. "Anyway, this works out much better. I was too busy to come anyway, so it's a good thing you came to me instead."

"I heard about the new house and I was curious," he admitted. "I did ask you to change, but I don't remember asking you to change this much, Mason."

"That's because you didn't. All that change… I didn't do it for you. I did it for myself, and for the woman I'm in love with."

With Dad, there was no point in mincing words, so I was just blurting everything as it came to mind. This was the man I'd learned confidence from though, and usually it was around him my confidence threatened to fail. There was always cracks in it, but what was behind the crack was the hurt, anger, and resentment.

Right then, it was only nervousness. In the end, it wouldn't matter to me whether he approved of us or not. I was determined to go along with my plans anyway. But it would be nice to receive his approval for once, so I wasn't always fighting against him, even if only in my head.

"Woman you're in love with?" Dad repeated, looking unfazed as he raised an eyebrow. "Well, that's certainly not something I expected from you. But I'm listening."

I hesitated to say more, and I actually had to muster the courage to get the words out. I decided to go the blunt route once more because it was something Dad appreciated.

"I've been dating someone," I said. "Her name is Laura and she's one of the maids at the hotel, though you probably don't know who she is. I plan to marry her, and this is the house I bought for us to live in."

I clamped my lips together before I overshared. Dad didn't need all the details about Laura and our life together. This much would be okay for him.

"I know who she is," Dad said, and it surprised me enough that I gaped at him. "You'd be surprised what I know about my employees, at least in this particular hotel. And she's friends with Emily, your sister has told me so much about her. Including how sick she was."

This was something I hadn't expected. My dad, who'd always preached to us about upholding the family tradition, was okay with my intention to marry a hotel maid? I would have thought it would take more convincing than this.

"So… you're really…"

"She's a good match," Dad continued, not waiting for me to finish. "From the little I know about her, and just how much you've changed since you started going out with this woman, she is definitely an excellent choice for you. I've always worried about you since you were young, Mason, but I also knew that you were going to make it."

He stepped closer to pat my arm, then walked slowly past me toward the house.

"I know you think I don't realize, or don't know… though there was certainly a lot I didn't know until I talked to Trent. I was hard on all of you boys, and in the end, it seems to have affected all of you negatively in ways I didn't expect. I didn't know what to do at the time, and the last thing I'd wanted was for you kids to grow up with regret. I know it might be a little late to ask forgiveness, but I've always been a father simply looking out for his children, in somewhat unorthodox ways. We aren't given a guidebook, you know, us parents?"

He began to walk towards the house as he spoke, not waiting for me to interrupt. I didn't have anything to argue back, and just followed him. In my time with Laura, I'd come to understand at least part of his behavior growing up. If Laura could forgive me for being controlling, then I could definitely do the same for Dad, especially when he looked like he was ready to change his dead-set ways.

We went into the house where I found Laura and Mom

sitting at the table together, both with pleasant looks on their faces.

"Honey, you're up," I said, walking closer and leaning down to give Laura a peck on the cheek. When Mom pouted at me, I sighed out a chuckle and gave her the same treatment.

"I'm supposed to be moving around little by little, not just staying in bed all day, you know," Laura returned with a roll of her eyes.

Everything with Laura was taken care of. She'd already had her surgery and gained her clean bill of health from her doctor, as promised. She was still recovering and gaining back her strength before she resumed her life fully, and as I'd promised, I'd stuck with her every step of the way.

"Laura and I are looking at wedding dresses," Mom said enthusiastically, holding up the tablet she held in her lap. "I'm sorry if I'm being too much, son, but your big brother is taking too long, and he might not even let me plan the wedding..."

I sighed, knowing Mom was saying it all that way just to bait me, and I knew I would let myself be baited anyway.

Emily had told her the moment I mentioned a proposal to her, and I was lucky enough that they didn't both blow it for me before I actually proposed. Emily had brought Mom to the hospital where she and Laura had first met. Laura was mostly embarrassed about the encounter, but the three women had become friendly after that. They were a perfect little foursome, with Trent's girlfriend, Jessi, who I finally got to meet. I was surprised to learn that she was the same

Jessi who'd grown up in the house with us. Her parents worked for my father and they'd always had their own quarters. I'd never really seen her much, but I knew who she was. What shocked me was learning she was a childhood friend of my brother.

I watched as Dad moved to sit beside Mom, and I moved to sit next to Laura. Where I'd once felt anger, I now only felt love. Where there had been fear, we all now had happiness. These were words she'd spoken to me before, and they meant everything in the picture that we painted. Time seemed to fly by as the four of us sat and chatted about the wedding, the house and Laura's positive influence on me, in what must have been the nicest conversation I'd had with my dad in a long time.

Later that evening, after my parents had left, as I was about to help Laura up so we could go to bed, she held me back with a hand on my arm.

"Is something wrong?" I asked, a little worried.

She shook her head with a serene smile, her hand flexing on my arm. "I just… wanted you to know something. At one point, I was so afraid at the idea of not living, and I let it rule my actions. I'm sorry, and I'm happy with how things are now. I'm not afraid anymore, and it's because I have you to look after me."

"Me and my family are a package deal," I warned, only half joking.

"And I don't mind it. You've compromised more than enough for me, especially since you quit partying," she said, teasing. Then her expression went serious. "You know what matters most in life, and I'm glad. So do I. This is an oath I made to myself after the first time I battled my illness, and I'll say it again for you to hear it, because I'm hoping it's something we can do together."

I waited as she took a deep breath to steady her breathing, my heart already going out to her and agreeing before she even let a word out of her mouth.

"I am going to take each day as it comes, and I am going to continue living to the fullest, out of joy, not fear. I'm going to face our future together with you, and I won't run away, no matter what."

With that little speech, I didn't think I'd have the patience to hold myself back from showing her that same promise. So I picked her up bridal style and carried my fiancée up the stairs to our bedroom to start on that bright future her words painted for us.

~ A billionaire revenge romance series ~
Twisted Beauty
Twisted Love
Twisted Fate

Mafia's Obsession

~ A hot mafia romance series ~
Mafia's Dirty Secret
Mafia's Fake Bride
Mafia's Final Play

Screaming Demons

~ An MC romance series full of suspense ~
Rough Start
Rough Ride
Rough Choice
Rough Patch
Rough Return
Rough Road
Rough Trip
Rough Night
Rough Love

Standalone Contemporary Romance

Billionaire in Vegas
Billionaire Hunt
Billionaire's Game
Billionaire Retreat
Billionaire On Air

A Chance To Love
Somebody To Love
Not Mine To Love

262

Check out Summer's entire collection at
www.summercooper.com/books

ABOUT SUMMER COOPER

Thank you so much for reading. Without you, it wouldn't be possible for me to be a full-time author. I hope you enjoy reading my books as much as I do writing them.

Besides (obviously!) reading and writing, I also love cuddling my dogs, shouting at Alexa, being upside down (aka Yoga) and driving my family cray-cray!

Get in touch at
hello@summercooper.com
www.summercooper.com

facebook.com/summercooperauthor
instagram.com/summercooperauthor
goodreads.com/summercooper
bookbub.com/profile/summer-cooper